MW01128145

1

Books By Jane O'Brien

The White Pine Trilogy

The Tangled Roots of Bent
Pine Lodge

The Dunes & Don'ts
Antiques Emporium

The Kindred Spirit Bed &
Breakfast

The Kindred Spirit

Bed & Breakfast

Bk 3 — The White Pine

Trilogy

Printed in the United States of America
Published by: Bay Leaf Publishing

Connect with Jane O'Brien

www.facebook.com/pages/Jane-OBrien

www.authorjaneobrien.com

Contact: authorjaneobrien@gmail.com

Dedication

This book is dedicated to my husband and best friend.   I often have to go to him for technical advice on things that are outside my scope of knowledge.   He listens patiently to my ramblings about the characters, makes suggestions about the settings, and he is the first one I allow to read my books.   I can always count on him for an honest critique about the storyline.   I couldn't have done this trilogy without his support.

Table of Contents

"Kindred spirits are not so scarce as I used to think.

It's splendid to find out there are so many of them in the world."

— L.M. Montgomery, Anne of Green Gables

PART ONE

Chapter One

"Will, I just don't know where you came up with this idea!" said Nora, getting more and more frustrated.   The argument had been going on for hours, now, and Will was not listening at all.

"Nora, I've already told you.   Please sit down so we can discuss this rationally, and I'll go over it one more time.   I need to tell you my thoughts without you pacing around the table. I can't think straight."

Nora sighed, took a pause to give Will a glaring stare, and then reluctantly sat down. She loved Will so much, but he had always been able to easily manipulate her.   He had a way with his words, and he knew how to be very charming; it seemed he always got what he wanted.   All he had to do was look into her eyes, and she reluctantly caved in.   She would have to be strong this time.   What he was proposing could change everything, but she wasn't sure she was ready for this big upheaval in her life right now.

"There," said Will, "that's better.   Can I get you some of your favorite tea?   It might help you relax."   He didn't wait for an answer, but jumped up and started to fill the teapot with water.   Once it was placed on the stove, he came back to the table and took both of Nora's hands in his.   She loved the warmth, and, as always, his touch went straight to her heart. The trouble was that he knew it.   He had always known how to use his charms on her, even back in high school when they were making out in the car and he had wanted to go a little farther than she had.   She could never win where Will was concerned. He was her weakness and therefore also her downfall.

"Okay," she said firmly, "you have exactly thirty minutes to state your case, and then I have to leave for work."

"And that right there is exactly why I've been wanting this change. We're always rushing from one place to another. There never seems to be time for us as a couple anymore. We each have different schedules, and we just pass each other on our way to and from work. Remember when we first got married how we would take Saturdays off and go for walks in the woods, or take long drives which usually ended at Lake Michigan with a stop at an ice cream shop? It was so nice to be with you without any distractions." Will looked deeply in Nora's eyes and held her gaze for as long as she would allow. When she pulled her eyes away, he began to shuffle some papers. He wanted to show her the figures and graphs he had come up with.

The pause was just enough time for Nora to get her bearings and to begin to formulate her thoughts.   His spell over her had been broken – for a while at least.

Will brushed his sandy-colored, unruly hair off his forehead with a quick swipe.   It did no good, of course, because it was always flyaway, looking as if he had just gotten out of bed and had forgotten to comb his hair. Brushing it back was a habit he had developed years ago, and one Nora had always thought endearing, but today, for some reason, she found it irritating.   But then again, when Will was focused on one of his crazy ideas or schemes and wouldn't back down, she often found him irritating.

"First of all," he said, "you know how I hate my job.   I only went into accounting because it was what my father wanted.   He had always planned for me to join his company and then someday take over when he was ready to retire.   I was to be the one to keep the family business going.   But there was one thing wrong with that idea – he forgot to ask me if it was what I wanted.   These past few years I've been miserable – I can't stand working at a desk all day.   Sometimes I feel like I am going to explode if I can't get outside and smell fresh air. You know all of this, already, Nor.   I really shouldn't have to say it again."   Will recognized his error the minute the shortened version of her name come out of his mouth.   It was what he had called her as teens, and she had hated it then, too.   He could see the narrowing of her eyes as she was about to remind him of it once again.   He decided to change the direction of the conversation quickly, so he pushed his papers towards her, and leaned in to explain what he had laid out.

"Okay, Will, I do understand that you never wanted to be trapped in an office building, but you went to college for accounting, just like he asked, and you didn't argue about it with your father then."

"I thought I could handle it. I wanted to please him, and he said if I followed in his footsteps, he would pay for my schooling one hundred percent; otherwise, I would have to get loans and grants wherever I could. I knew my grades weren't good enough for scholarships, so I thought I would just get through college, letting him cover it, and figure out my life later. Then after we got married, we needed the regular income, and I found myself stuck with seemingly no way out. But this is my chance – our chance! Nora, hear me out, please."

Nora could no longer resist the pleading look in Will's eyes, and she didn't want the financial struggles of their marriage to be the reason for his misery, so she decided to try her hardest to see his point of view. "Okay, I'll try to keep an open mind this time, but just get on with it. Time is running out," she said glancing at the clock on the wall.

"As you know, it came up in conversation with my buddy Chase Phillips that the old Taylor mansion is for sale in Taylor Ridge. I've always had a fascination for that place. When we were kids, the place was empty one time when it was in between owners. On occasion we were able to sneak inside and explore. I loved roaming the rooms and wondering what it must have been like to live there when it was first built. I didn't know a thing about history, but I knew it must have been a long time ago. I imagined how it would have looked and dreamed of restoring it to its former glory when I grew up. And now we have that chance. Because of the market, we can buy it for a song. The time is now or never."

"But, Will, the place must need a lot of repairs, and you're not a carpenter or, sorry, even a handyman in any way. It just doesn't make sense."

Will had a hurt look at her comment on what kind of a man he was.   He did not see himself in the same light.   He was no expert, but he could surely swing a hammer or use a screwdriver when necessary.   He actually knew the difference between a flathead screwdriver and a Phillips; and he also knew what an Allen wrench was.   That vocabulary gave him something to throw around when talking to the guys.   He forged ahead, trying to ignore her remark.   "It's been run as a bed and breakfast for the last ten years.   I'm sure in a house that size and that old there's always going to be something that needs repair, but for the most part, it has been functioning as a prosperous business.   The owners are ready to retire to Florida permanently.   They've already left for the season.   It's actually move-in ready, so that's nice.   And anything that needs fixing up, we can do along the way.   Look, here is the profit and loss sheet from last year they provided. The Realtor faxed it to me."

Nora looked at the bottom line where it showed net income, looked up, and said, "Are you crazy? We can't live on that, especially once I give up my job!"

"But honey, you forgot one thing. I *am* an accountant. I can see that there are a lot of things here that should be write-offs, things the previous owners were missing. And just think about the fact that we will be living in our place of business. Therefore, all expenses belong to the business. We won't need as much gas for the car because we'll be working from home, and even when we drive to the grocery store, we can deduct the mileage because we'd also be stocking up on food for the B&B. There are so many benefits to having a business in your home it's unbelievable, so we really wouldn't need the income that we are depending on now."

He really had thought all of this through. Nora was surprised at the intensity of his passion for this idea. This was something completely different than all of the other schemes he had come up with, but there was one big problem. Nora didn't cook.

"Will, it's a bed and breakfast, right? What about breakfast? You know me in the kitchen. I can make a few meals that my mother made when I was a kid, but I'm not into fancy dishes, and wouldn't that be what people would expect?"

"Not always. All B&Bs are different. Some offer more home-style cooking. It can be whatever you want it to be. I'll let you decide. You can be the overall general manager, and since I love people, I'll be the greeter and book the guests."

"I agree that working from home would be nice. I'm not crazy about my job, either, but there's a lot more to it than you're making out. What about the maintenance needs? As far as I know you know nothing about plumbing. What if a pipe breaks?"

Will sensed that she was starting to come around; his heart began to race.   "I agree that I'm not a great handyman, but I can fix most things temporarily, and as soon as we start turning a better profit than the last folks, we can afford to hire professional contractors.   You have a real talent for decorating, and just think of all of the quilts you can make for the beds! Together you and I can make the Taylor mansion a showplace!"   Will saw Nora's look and knew then he had finally hit on the right thing - quilts.

Nora began to think of all of the free time she would have to spend sewing, and because it was for the business, she wouldn't have to feel guilty that she was taking time away from her daily chores.   Of course, there would be routine housecleaning, but she was always pretty good at doing that quickly.   Maybe this could work, she thought.   Was it possible that he had actually worked it out more than she had given him credit for?   It seemed that Will had certainly thought of everything.   Still, she had her reservations.

"I understand what you're saying, but I don't want to move on this too fast.   We need to take a ride up there and look the place over. We have to be very careful and not view it through your eyes as you did when you were a child, but from a business perspective.   Things might be quite different there than they were the last time you were in Taylor Ridge."

Will jumped up and grabbed Nora, spinning her around.   "Thank you, honey. Thank you, thank you!   Thank you for giving it a chance.   That area of Michigan is so beautiful; I know you're going to love it."

"Hold on.   I didn't say yes, yet.   And if – and that's a big if – I like it, we'll need to have it completely inspected by a licensed professional. I've never been too fond of this apartment, and city living is not my thing, but it is a good life, Will, and I don't want to throw it away carelessly. But I promise to look with an open mind, and that's as far as I'm willing to go at this point."

"Okay, I understand. I'll make the call to the Realtor today and set up an appointment. We'll go soon and check it out. No pressure, I promise." He leaned in for an Eskimo kiss, rubbing noses the way they had done since they were teens, and then he kissed her properly, a kiss she could feel to her toes. Nora sighed; she knew she was in trouble now, because she loved nothing more than making Will happy.

"I have to leave for work. We'll talk more tonight. When the Realtor has a date to show the place, we can coordinate our schedules. See you later." Nora gave Will another quick kiss, grabbed her car keys, and went out the door. Oh my, she thought, what have I agreed to now?

Nora Carter was a manager in a department store in the mall called Fancy's. She didn't mind it, but it certainly wasn't her dream job.   She was in charge of keeping the employees in line, training new help, and basically keeping things running smoothly -- which it almost never did.   The turnover rate was unbelievable.   The young people these days left their jobs whenever the smallest thing bothered them.   Just the other day she had told Becky, her new employee in training, that gum chewing was not allowed on the floor.   Becky claimed it calmed her nerves, and it was a habit she could not break.   She insisted she could keep her juicy wad in the corner of her cheek and no one would know it was there. Impossible, said Nora.   So Becky had thrown her badge down on the counter and walked off, just like that!   Then there was Sara who couldn't stop texting even when she was told over and over to leave her phone in her locker before coming into the jean department, which was her area to cover. She insisted she only texted a few words here and there, and it couldn't possibly hurt anyone. Nora had had to ask her to leave since she would not cooperate. For the most part, they were part-time help throughout the school year and into summer, and she was sure they were just there to please their parents. Not one of them really needed the money.

Well, that wasn't completely true, she had to admit; Penny was the best. She said her paycheck was a necessity, and she had to turn most of it over to her single mom to help with the younger kids. Apparently, there was no financial help at all from the missing, deadbeat father. She was a real sweet girl - shy and humble, and she always came to work on time. She did whatever was asked of her, and she never complained.   Nora wished they would all be like Penny, but she knew girls like Penny only came along once in a blue moon.

So far, Nora's day was progressing routinely.   There were the usual noisy children running up and down the aisles, the returns when she was almost positive the item had been worn already, and the rejected credit cards which always shocked and embarrassed their owners.   She would smile and assure the person that it must just be a problem with the system and ask them to come again after they had worked out the glitches.   For the most part, Nora took it all in her stride, but being locked up in a building with no windows was just as awful for her as it was for Will.   She never cared for enclosed spaces; they made her feel trapped. But this job had come along right when they needed it most.   The pay was not the greatest, but it did supplement Will's income, and their nest egg had been building at a steady pace.

Nora and Will had gotten married when he was in his first year of college. They eloped when, one crazy night, Will convinced her he just had to live with her on a regular basis. He knew his family would never go along with them moving in together any other way. But the biggest problem was that his father almost cut off all the funding to college once he heard the news. He eventually gave in on the tuition, but he insisted they pay for their own housing and utilities. Nora now understood that Will's Dad had dealt with his impulsive behavior all of his life and was just trying to encourage him to become a responsible adult. But being married had created havoc in their finances and Nora had had to drop out of college and get a job to keep them going, and even with her income, they were constantly struggling. They refused to give up on their plan to always save ten percent, which they had regularly set aside and viewed as being untouchable.   They made concessions in other ways.

Nora thought about Will's idea all day long.   She finally had to admit to herself that going further into debt, by owning a bed and breakfast, as crazy as that sounded, might be their only way of bettering themselves.   So by the end of her shift she had decided to give Will the go-ahead if the house passed inspection. For now, though, she would let Will think she was still mulling the idea over, just in case the property was a disaster.   And if it was, she would be firm; there would absolutely be no bed and breakfast in the picture for them.

Chapter Two

The Realtor had called and said the house would be available for viewing on Saturday. Will was as excited as a little boy on Christmas morning.   Nora was still keeping her feelings in check so she wouldn't be swept away with his enthusiasm.   The drive from Lima, Ohio would be a long one, so they decided to make a weekend of it.   They planned to get an early start, and then after viewing the house, they would find a motel to stay in overnight, before coming home Sunday morning.

When Saturday finally rolled around, which later turned out to be a beautiful spring morning, they were both up before the sun rose.

They quickly packed some snacks in a soft-sided cooler, filled their travel mugs with coffee, and took some bottles of water from the fridge for the road.   Nora realized that Will had been right about the trip; it felt like a much-needed vacation, and she could feel her worries sliding off her back like a sheet of ice melting in the sun with each mile they traveled.

When they first crossed into Michigan, they noticed that the scenery hadn't changed at all.   The trees, the roadside weeds, the farmlands and farmhouses all looked alike, just as God had intended – a land with no borders. But something strange happened as soon as they drove north of Grand Rapids and started to leave the city behind.   The landscape was rolling with gentle waves of hills and valleys.   The white pine and oak were growing more densely together.   The early spring wildflowers on the roadside added bright splotches of color amidst the tall grasses, and there seemed to be more bird activity flying overhead, especially the hawks who dove for field mice and rabbits, sometimes coming dangerously close to the car. They saw ducks and swans slowly swimming in the rivers and streams which flowed gently under the many bridges they crossed. The waterfowl seemed so relaxed, almost in a lazy daze, and soon Nora was, too.

After a few hours, they left the expressway and started to drive on a two-lane highway heading west toward the shore of Lake Michigan. They had agreed to take the back roads as soon as possible so they could appreciate the layout of the land as they headed toward Ludington. And then, after a few gas and potty stops, they finally came to a sign announcing their arrival in the community of Taylor Ridge.

"Let's pull over here in the roadside park, and get our bearings," said Will with a big grin on his face.

"I'd like that," agreed Nora, with a yawn. "I need to stretch my legs.   Look, there's an overlook of some kind; let's walk over and check it out."

Will got out of the car and came around to Nora's side.   He put his arm around her and gently kissed her on the cheek.   "Thanks for giving this a try, Nora.   And if it doesn't work out, at least we'll have a nice weekend together."

Nora smiled at him and laid her head on his shoulder for a second.   She truly loved Will with all of her heart.   He was always so sweet. They walked toward the edge of the overlook and stood next to a sign that proclaimed this to be a 'scenic view.'   "Oh, my, it's beautiful.   Look how far we can see from here," said Nora.

Will leaned over the safety railing trying to take it all in.   "The river is a long way down, isn't it?   I wish we had time to take the walk down to the riverbank.   That sign said there were 335 steps.   We should come back another time and give it a try."

They stood at the railing, side by side, with the sun warming their backs and enjoyed the sight.   They were looking at treetops on the opposite bank, and it was nothing but green as far as the eye could see.   The smell of pine permeated the air, a fragrance that Nora would learn to love.

"Breathe deeply, Nora.   We could be smelling this fresh air for the rest of our lives, God willing.   This could be the beginning of a whole new life for us.   Let's pray that the house is in good condition, and then we can make a proper decision."   Will inhaled and exhaled, savoring the sweet air.   "Gosh, I hate to leave this peaceful place right now, but we have to meet the Realtor, and I'm not quite sure how much farther we have to go."

"Okay," said Nora reluctantly.   "We can check the GPS for travel time when we get in the car."

They quickly discovered they were closer than they thought; they only needed to go a few short miles, and then suddenly, they were in the small village of Taylor Ridge.   The buildings were old but all seemed to be well-kept.   Many had brick facades and had a look of the turn of the twentieth century.   There was the usual gas station, post office and hardware store, along with a few other necessary businesses needed for a small town to function, like a pharmacy, a small grocery store, dollar store, and oil change business, and an automotive repair shop.   One block seemed to be devoted to antiques shops, gift shops, and a fabric shop advertising quilt fabric.   An arrow pointed to a Lutheran church on one corner and an Episcopal church on another corner.   Farther down was a Methodist church; their sign proclaimed they were holding a pot luck on Sunday.   And on the next corner sat a Baptist church, which was putting on a craft sale on an upcoming weekend.   A large wooden sign announced that the Lion's Club met on Tuesday night at 7:00 p.m., and the Rotary Club sponsored the Little League and maintained the park.

"There's no shortage of churches here," noticed Nora. "I guess that's a good sign. Maybe that means the town is full of moral and God-fearing people. I don't suppose we'll see any gangs wearing colors, and hopefully not much drug traffic."

"That's one of the things I remember about living here when I was young. Everyone went to church and all the kids went to Sunday school. And vacation Bible school was the highlight of the summer. Church camp was the place most pre-teens were able to sneak their first kiss." Will had a faraway look as he recalled the days of being a kid in Taylor Ridge. He was able to ride his bike wherever he wanted, and he remembered being gone for hours and no one even questioned him about it, as long as he was home in time for supper. He would grab his fishing pole, yelling to his mother as he ran out the door, 'Goin' fishing,' and then he'd head to the pond with his buddies. They usually didn't catch anything big enough to keep, but the fun was simply hanging out together and talking about what they would do with their lives when they were grownups. When Will's parents told him they were moving to Ohio and he would have to leave Chase, Ben, and Ted behind, he had cried for hours. He couldn't imagine ever having such good friends as those three guys. But looking back he now knew it had been the best thing financially for his family, and if he hadn't moved, he would never have met Nora.

"Nora, if we have time, is it all right if I look up the guys?"

"Sure, I don't see why not. We might as well meet some locals. But be prepared, Will, people change as the years go by; they might not be the same as when they were kids. I know you've kept in contact with Chase, but Ben and Ted could be completely different than you remember."

"I understand, but I wouldn't be able to live with myself if I didn't at least try to contact them.   We'll wait until we see what kind of time we have left.   Maybe we can meet them for dinner or something."

"Sounds like a plan."   Nora had tried to be as agreeable as possible so Will would know that she was truly giving his idea some thought. There was no sense in complaining about it; otherwise he would not take her seriously if she said she didn't want to go along with the whole bed and breakfast idea.

They were supposed to meet Nancy Garvey, the real estate agent, at 1:00 at the mansion and it was already 12:30.   They had planned to arrive a little early in order to get a view of the place without any pressure or comments from her, expecting that she would be persuasive and might try to skew their judgment.   Will plugged in the address at 3010 Red Oak Lane, and they headed toward their destination, forgoing lunch in order to arrive before Nancy.

"I'm glad we brought snacks.   I'm starting to get hungry," said Will, glancing over the back seat.   "Can you reach the bag with the goodies, hon?"

"Sure.   How about a granola bar? They're not messy and should carry you for a few hours."

"Great.   Hand over."   Will stretched out his hand as he kept his eyes on the road.   They began to leave the downtown area on Fernwood Avenue, and then the road took them up quite a steep hill.   "There's the street sign already, Red Oak Lane.   That's good.   It's not too far off the beaten path; for a business to be successful, it should be easy to find and near other activities."

"The GPS says it's on the right just a little way ahead," said Nora, looking out the window and trying to read mailbox addresses. "Holy cow! Are you kidding me? This is it?" Will grinned knowing it had made the impact on Nora that he had expected.

She was in awe at the sight of the house perched up high on a grass-covered dune at the top of a long driveway. This was a house that was truly worthy of being called a mansion. It was a large Greek revival, maybe the largest one Nora had ever seen. The two-story had a cupola with a widow's walk on top of the roof; the view from there was bound to be spectacular. It was painted white but the paint was peeling badly, giving it a shabby, un-cared for look. The windows were dirty, but that was to be expected with no one living in it at the moment, and the grass and hedges needed trimming, contributing to the unkempt feel, and giving it

an eerie vibe.   Nora had never believed in
ghosts so that wouldn't bother her in the least,
but she could see that people would be turned
off by the house's appearance.   The large sign
out front stating this to be the Taylor Mansion
Bed & Breakfast was badly in need of some fresh
paint, or more likely should be replaced.   Nora
realized she was already fixing up the exterior in
her head, and found herself imagining how she
could landscape the grounds to give it a
welcoming look.   Suddenly, she had an
overwhelming desire to get inside.

    An older model Mercedes pulled up
behind them as they came to a stop in front of
the massive front porch.   Its tires crunched on
the gravel drive, and then the driver's door
opened as a woman emerged.   She appeared to
be about 50, but it was difficult to tell as her face
was wrinkle-free; she could be quite a bit older.
She was perfectly groomed in a skirted, peach-
colored business suit, which complimented her

silver-white hair. She greeted them with a bright smile, introducing herself with ease and confidence. Obviously, she's done this more than a few times before, thought Nora.

"Will and Nora? I'm Nancy. So nice to meet you both," she said. "It's a beautiful day, isn't it? I hope you had a pleasant trip."

"We did," said Will. "It was a very enjoyable ride, but I'm afraid I missed a lot of the scenery, because I was so focused on getting to see the house."

"Well, then, let's get started," said Nancy. "Would you like to go inside first or walk the grounds?"

"I'm all for going in," said Nora, with a racing heart. She hadn't anticipated being this excited. If she was feeling like this, she could only imagine how Will was feeling. A quick glance at him told her he was on the same page. He winked and then took her hand as they climbed the seven wide steps to the front door.

The porch floor was made of a wide planked board and was painted the usual porch gray.   It was large enough to hold several pieces of furniture so the guests could sit on the porch in the evening to catch a nice breeze, which most likely would come from the west off Lake Michigan.

"I'm sure you noticed the huge white columns going straight up to the second floor. It's one of the focal points of this house, and the main point of the architectural design that denotes a Greek revival.   Another point, if you notice, is the long rectangular windows, of which there are many, all across the front.   It was a very popular design in the 1850s, but most homes weren't this grand.   Now, let me see if I can figure out this lock box so I can retrieve the key."   She punched in a few numbers and the box that was hanging on the door knob popped open; she then removed the key and unlocked the door, which was heavy and very tall.   It had a large rectangular glass window that caught the light and above it there was a half-circle, sunburst window in a beautiful leaded glass pattern.   On each side of the door were two "sidelights" as Nancy explained they were called by builders; they were actually not lights at all, but windows that ran from the top of the door to the floor, and they were in the same leaded glass pattern as the rest.   Nora knew a little about architecture because she loved looking at home decorating magazines.   Since they were just apartment dwellers, Will had always teased her about her dreams of high-style living.

"Absolutely beautiful."   Nora was now staring at the staircase in awe.

Nancy chuckled.   "You have the exact same reaction that most people have when they enter the house."

"Wow, Nora, can you believe this?   It looks so much different than when I was a kid. I remember the curving staircase coming down from both sides, but I guess when I was young, I didn't really pay much attention to the detail in the woodwork." Will was caressing the newel post and studying the carving. A scene of birds and vines ran from the base to the cap of the post. He checked it all over to see if it was intact, and then went to the other side to do the same. "Well, at least it's in good condition. It would be quite difficult to repair something like that."

"Oak is a very common wood used for woodwork in homes in this area. It was plentiful and therefore cheap, but besides that, it's a hardwood and it lasts forever. The original owner was a lumber magnate, so he spared no expense when building this home in what was at that time almost a wilderness. He wanted to make his mark on the world, so the other settlers would recognize who was in power and control, here. Come this way and we can go into the parlor." Nancy gestured with a sweep of her arm that they should follow; she continued with her tour voice. "The previous owner used this sitting room for the guests to congregate and relax."

"Oh, my," said Nora feeling silly with all of her comments and exclamations. She felt a little like a child at her first fireworks display with all of her 'oohs' and 'aahs,' but it couldn't be helped -- the exclamations seemed to come out of her mouth without her consent.

The tour of the many rooms actually took them an hour and a half as they stopped to discuss some history and inspect certain details in the construction. Both Nora and Will were pleased to see that the kitchen had been modernized with commercial-grade appliances, so passing inspection for the bed and breakfast should be no problem. It had been upgraded with a new white subway tile as a backsplash, giving that old feel while still looking shiny and clean. The countertop was a beautiful soft grey granite, which went beautifully with the stainless appliances.   Very professional looking.   Nora thought maybe she would paint the walls a new pastel color just to put her own stamp on it. Color wheels were already spinning in her head.

The views from the upstairs windows in the eight bedrooms were breathtaking, but it was the enclosed widow's walk above the second floor that got most of Nora's attention.   From that high vantage point they could stand in the center of the small area and make a 360-degree turn, seeing over the whole town and out to the Lake.   Nora could also view the woods which began at the edge of the wide expanse of lawn. The yard rolled gently down from the back of the house to a small pond, and there was a charming, black, wrought iron gazebo sitting at its edge.

"Will, look at the gazebo.   I've dreamed of owning one like this my whole life.   There always seems to be something special and romantic about a gazebo."

"Nora, have you thought about what you could do with this room?   Look at all of the light coming from the windows.   It would make a perfect – "

"--sewing room," Nora said finishing his sentence.   "You're absolutely right.   It is perfect.   This could be my very own room, so I wouldn't have to have fabric scraps all over the counters and kitchen table.   Now you've got my attention," she laughed as she turned to Nancy. "But what is that building over there?"   On the far right of the property next to a long row of white pines was a glass building with vines growing over it.

"That's the greenhouse.   I don't think the previous owners ever did anything with it.   It looks like it has some broken and cracked glass, but I suppose it could be easily repaired if you had a use for it.

"I would love to try greenhouse

gardening," said Nora, "but I can see that that project would have to take a back seat to many others that will be on a list of things that need to be done."

"Of course," agreed Nancy. "There's not a lot to do as far as decorating, and for the most part, it's a well-maintained house, so it would be totally up to you as far as how much you wanted to bring it up-to-date. That's a big money saver, right there. A lot of times, people want to start a B&B, and they have to totally gut a house from top to bottom. It takes a long time to recover your money that way, and it's sometimes years before a profit can be made. With this home, you would be buying into an existing business, with an impressive client list and an active website. That's a big plus."

Will had been taking notes, and jotting down cost estimates. This would be a bigger job than he had first anticipated, because he knew Nora wouldn't stop until she had created a masterpiece, but she was actually coming around to the idea.   He couldn't believe it!

"Well," he said, "I can see that we won't be able to handle running this place on our own. We're definitely going to need to hire help. And, I'm thinking that we'll most likely have to close the business for a few months while we renovate.   Did you bring the books and spreadsheets, and the owner's latest profit and loss statement that I asked to look at?   I'm going to need to verify income, et cetera, before we can commit to anything."

"Yes, I have them with me in my briefcase.   I think you're going to like what you see," said Nancy.

Will and Nancy sat at a table and began going over facts and figures that were way over Nora's head.   She was glad that Will understood it all, because she surely didn't, and in fact, she didn't want to.   She would have to trust Will in that area.   Studying numbers was his profession, and according to his father he was darn good at it, whether he liked what he did for a living or not.   So while they were absorbed in what Nora considered to be the boring part of business, she continued to roam the rooms to get a better feel of the place without the constant chatter and Nancy's sales pitch in the background.

Nora moved from bedroom to bedroom, once again exploring all of the nooks and crannies.   Most of the rooms were quite large according to today's standards but that might be because there were no closets.   Each room had an armoire to hold clothing.   As in the case of most bed and breakfasts, guests would have to share one of two bathrooms down the hall.   At the time this house had been built, indoor plumbing didn't even exist, so at some point the bathrooms had been added, meaning that more bedrooms had had to be sacrificed for this luxury.   Nora wondered if a small bath with a shower only could be added in each room so the guests would not have to walk down the hall at night before retiring.

Nora felt that something about this house, or mansion as it was called around here, was very comforting. Even though it was huge and a person could easily get turned around their first time or two, it still had a homey vibe. Maybe it was because of all of the antiques that had been left behind. They were quite formal but still looked as if they had been used regularly and therefore didn't appear to be too delicate. A person would not be afraid to sit in a chair, and in a bed and breakfast that was important. There was also an occasional manly leather chair perfectly placed so as to fit the décor -- no doubt, a concession to the man who just can't get his head wrapped around why anyone would want to stay in a B&B, but was probably there strictly to please his wife or partner. That's good, thought Nora, a guest should never feel uncomfortable. Her next question for Nancy will be: Are they taking all of the furnishings. Filling this place with furniture and area rugs, would be very costly.

She roamed down the stairs again, and turned to her left. That was what Nancy had said would have been the room that was reserved for family. The parlor would have always been kept neat and tidy for company, but here in this room, the family could sit by the fire and share events of their day after dinner, maybe the children would be on the floor playing quietly while their parents talked.

Off of the sitting room and through French doors, was a glorious room that she had almost missed. The sunroom. Nora stood in the center and tried to get her bearings as far as north and south were concerned. Yes, the window wall along the end was facing the east. That would have been perfect to let in the morning light. The sun must warm the room but not allow it to get too hot, so the guests could have their breakfasts out here on good days. Then she turned slightly to the right and looked out the wall of glass there. This side was facing the south. That could be trouble on a hot day, raising the temperatures in this room and making it unusable, except for one thing -- a beautiful, majestic white pine. It would block out the heat of the day and still allows plenty of light to come in. The bird activity in this tree would be fantastic. Just as Nora had that thought, a gorgeous red cardinal swooped into the branches and disappeared. Nora hoped it was tending to a nest. That would be exciting to watch!

Nora could tell by the volume and inflection of voices coming from the other room, that Will and Nancy were winding up their discussion, so she walked back to the room where she had left them. Will was saying, "Thank you so much for your time, Nancy.

Nora and I have a lot to talk about, and we'd like to roam the property if you don't mind.   We're going to stay in town for the weekend and get a good look around.   And you can bet we'll be talking of nothing else but this house."

"Yes, I really appreciate the tour," said Nora.   "I didn't hear the asking price, and I'm almost afraid to ask, but I guess you gave Will all of the details.   I have a feeling it's way beyond our budget, but we'll get back to you one way or the other, as soon as we can."

"I understand.   But don't take too long to make up your mind.   That's a great price for what you get, and I don't think it will last long, once the word gets out about it being for sale. People in this town are very proud and protective about their local mansion and all of the history that goes with it.   If you decide to take it, I'll fill you in on some of the details – those I know of, anyway."

"Okay, great.   We're going to look up

some of Will's buddies and try to meet them for lunch or dinner.   Then we will be crunching numbers, I'm sure.   Oh, and can you recommend a good motel?" asked Nora.

"There's one on the north side of town back on the old highway.   Go back to Fernwood Avenue and turn right.   It's just a few miles up the road.   Now, let me see if I can operate this lockbox once more.   They always seem to be so tricky.   There, that does it.   Easier than I thought.   Nice to have met you, and here's my card.   You can call my cell or my home phone. I'll be around all weekend; I just live five miles east of here."

They said their goodbyes and Nancy drove off, leaving Will and Nora in the driveway to stare at the house for a few minutes more.   "I really like it, Will.   I'm surprised, but I really, really like – no, I love it!   And now that I've fallen in love with it, I'm afraid we probably can't afford it."

"Let's take it one step at a time," grinned Will. "When I have a good look at the numbers and lay it out for you, you'll see, but I'm pretty sure we can swing it."

Nora could see how happy Will was, and she had to admit that she was, too. Was it possible? Would they actually be owners of a bed and breakfast soon? Will was such a positive thinker, and he always said anything was possible. Today for the first time, she actually believed he was right.

Chapter Three

Will and Nora spent another half hour walking the property, or part of it at least. They discovered a small creek running through the woods that Will said was known as Briar Creek. It was a minor tributary to the Platte River which then flowed into Lake Michigan. There was some good fishing to be had here, he had said excitedly, as his face lit up with anticipation. Finally it was time to leave, and as they drove down the driveway, Nora felt a very strong pull back to the house. She turned around in her seat for one last look, and felt an overwhelming desire to go back 'home'—this house, not her apartment. She had never experienced anything like it in her life. She knew at that moment, that no matter what numbers Will came up with, she was all in. It could be the best thing or the worst thing that ever happened to her, but she knew she had to find out.

The drive to the motel was easy and just a few minutes away. That was also a good sign, because as Will pointed out, if they could develop a relationship with the owners, they could send guests back and forth whenever one of them was already booked for the night.

"Here it is," said Will with his fake cheerful voice.

The motel was the total opposite of a bed and breakfast. It was a painted brick, one-story building, with about ten rooms. It was obvious from the outside that it was strictly a place to lay your head on a pillow for the night. It needed a new coat of paint, and even though the grass had been cut, no one had bothered to trim the weeds close to the building and around the tree trunks.

Branches from several bushes stuck out at odd angles.

"Um, do we really want to go in there?" asked Nora, thinking a bad night was around the corner.

"Let's ask to see a room before we pass judgment.   But I really don't see another option other than starting to drive towards home and trying to find something else along the way."

Nora raised an eyebrow and looked at him skeptically.   She was easy going about most things, but motel rooms was not one of them. The thought that some stranger had recently slept in the same bed that she was about to crawl into, had always been a little unnerving.   "Okay, let's have a code word for 'I don't like it.'   How about 'get me out of here.'?"

"Come on, Nora.   It can't be that bad. It looks like other people stay here all the time. You're just used to the way they do things in a bigger city."

"Okay, let's take a look, but just a warning -- I'm not opposed to sleeping in the car."

Will went into the office while Nora waited outside.   It gave her a chance to look around a little.   There really wasn't much to see here, but plenty of nature.   White pines were everywhere, along with several other types of pine trees that she didn't recognize.   If they were to move here, she would have to get a book about the trees of Michigan in order to learn more about her new surroundings.   She was sure they probably had some of the same trees in Ohio, but she had never paid that much attention to them before, other than in the spring when a tree bloomed with pink or white blooms in a business's landscaping or along a parkway.   She was suddenly eager to learn more about nature and plants.

Will emerged from the office followed by an elderly gentleman with a bunch of keys dangling in his hand.   He motioned for her to follow them.   "Nora, this is Mr. Reed.   He's the owner of the Sand and Pines Motel."

"How do you do, Mr. Reed.?"

Mr. Reed nodded at her and walked toward a room.   Nora noticed that he either had trouble with his hips or had had a hip replacement.   His gait was a little like a penguin waddling on slippery ice.   "Will tells me you young folks are looking at the mansion," he said, while fussing with the keys to the door for Room 12.   "Quite an undertaking for someone your age.   I'd do it in a minute if I was younger and I still had my Maggie with me.   She was a real people-person, I tell ya'.   Always had cookies and doughnuts out for the guests.   We had quite a few regulars, and I swear they came just to see her.   And she kept the rooms spotless. Nowadays, I hire my granddaughter to clean for me, and getting the chores done around the yard is almost impossible for me.   There it goes. That lock is always a little sticky."

He pushed the door open and stepped aside so they could enter first. The room was sparse, but surprisingly bright and clean. Not a trace of mildew or cigarette smell in the air, as Nora had feared. Will checked out the channels on the TV while Nora walked to the bathroom and pulled back the shower curtain. It was sparkling and fresh, as were the mirrors which were squeaky clean and streak-free. The pile on the carpet around the bed was raised, making a cross-hatched pattern, evidence of having been recently vacuumed. Everything looked newly dusted. What a nice surprise.

"You won't find a bit of dirt in here, Miss. My granddaughter, Sally, is a perfectionist. I tease her about it, because she takes so long to clean a room after a checkout."

"It's very nice, Mr. Reed. You can tell her she is doing an excellent job." Nora smiled at him, and gave Will a little nod.

"Okay, we'll take it. We only need it for

one night, but if things go the way I think they might, it could be our home away from home for a little while."

Mr. Reed smiled and said, "Follow me, young man.   Let's get the paperwork done."

As soon as they were settled in their room, Will and Nora studied his notes, and made comments from their observations.   Will went over spreadsheets and he discussed costs of operation, which included repair, maintenance, payroll, and insurances.   Just like previously in their apartment, Nora's head began to swim with the numbers, and she started to zone out.   She found herself daydreaming about actually being a business owner and being the one who controlled her day.   Together they could call the shots, even if that meant that sometimes pressure would be put on them to generate an income.

"Will, I'm sure you have this thing all

65

figured out, but believe me, it means nothing to me.   I hear you, but it just doesn't make sense to my numbers-dead brain."   Nora placed her elbows on the table and her chin in her hand. "I guess, I'm more concerned about how it will impact our marriage.   Can we work well together?   I've heard all kinds of horror stories about husband-and-wife business ventures."

Will thought a minute and then said carefully, "As long as we map out our areas of expertise, and give each person leeway and respect in that area, I think we can handle it quite well.   For instance, you will be in charge of the decorating, and either cleaning the rooms yourself or hiring the cleaning crew and managing them.   I'll take over the maintenance, repairs, and outdoor work.   I will also have to hire whatever I can't do myself, but you won't have to deal with that part, at all. We can share booking and greeting the guests."

"Sounds good so far, but it *is* a bed and

breakfast.   I'm pretty terrified of the breakfast part," replied Nora.   "But I'm up for learning, if you'll give me a chance.   I'll have to round up a few recipes and try them out first."

"That's the spirit, Nora.   I'll even be your guinea pig."   Will made a face at her and then clutched his stomach as if he was about to fall over from food poisoning.   Laughing together was good for them.   They wiped their eyes, took a few deep breaths to stop the giggles, and went back to their talk.

"Seriously, Nora, we'll give them all a try, and then make them over and over again to make sure the results are always the same.   I'll even help with the baking until you get the hang of it.   You'll only need a few items on the menu, and remember most people only come once.   If they do return, it's usually months or even a year before they come back.   So you can serve the same thing every weekend, and no one will be any the wiser."

"Yes, I guess, you're right.   I think I can handle that.   Next is the financing.   I'm worried about that.   Do you think the owners will come down in price?   What about our down payment for the mortgage?   Do you think we have enough?   We'd need to hold back some savings for the upkeep."

And on and on it went.   Once they decided they had covered all of the bases, and felt they had reached an agreement, they decided to call it quits for the day.

"I'm exhausted," said Will.   "Let's give one of the guys a call and see if we can meet up somewhere.   We never had any lunch, and it's really getting late.   We're working our way into dinnertime already."

"Okay, call first, set a time if we can, and then let's get a short nap in."

"Maybe more than just a nap?"   Will raised an eyebrow, grinned, and tackled his lovely wife onto the bed.

Chapter Four

Will tried contacting Chase with the number he had on his cell phone, hoping it was still working. He had not used it in quite a while. Chase was one of those friends that he didn't need to talk to often to feel a closeness to. As soon as they re-connected, no matter how much time had passed, they fell back into their banter and laughter, as they recalled old times. Surprisingly, the phone number was still working and Chase answered immediately. He was thrilled to find out that Will and Nora were in town, and eagerly agreed to meet them in a half hour for a late lunch at The Lite House, a favored sandwich shop of the locals. The

House, as it was called by those who frequented it, was only open for lunch and dinner, and served quick, light fare.   Chase was self-employed and could make his own hours, so it was no problem for him to get time off, but as he explained, the other guys had regular day jobs. They might not be able to make it.   He would call Ted and Ben and see what he could do to get them there.

Will was elated at having a chance to get together with at least Chase and maybe the others also.   He encouraged Nora to hurry with her shower and get dressed so they could be there on time.   But Nora was never one to rush through her routine.   She had learned to pace herself, and therefore was normally never late for anything.   Will on the other hand would usually fly through his shower, then towel dry his hair with a flurry, which is most probably why it was always so fly-away.   He'd yank up his pants, hop on one foot and then the other

70

while trying to get his shoes and socks on, and then wait impatiently for Nora, sighing and tapping his fingers on the TV remote. He could never understand why she did not moving faster.

Nora studied herself in the mirror. She blew out her long, medium-brown, hair to gentle waves. She studied her eyes closely as she applied mascara and eye liner to enhance her already stunning golden eyes. She had been told by more than one person, that with that eye color and their slight almond shape, she had eyes like a cat. Nora took pride in the fact that she had a unique look, although she had never considered herself to be beautiful. When she was a teen, she just wanted to look like the blonde cheerleaders with their bouncy ponytails, but she soon realized that was not happening for her. Her wise mother had explained that she should make the most of what she had and had taught her how to enhance her facial features. As she grew older and became more practiced at the art of makeup, Nora had been able to transform herself into a real beauty.   Now, she never went out of the house without applying some degree of eye makeup and lipstick.   And of course, even though Will was always impatient, he whole-heartedly approved of the results.

"Oh, baby, you look like dessert.   If only we weren't going out right now, we could have another round of fun!"

"Will, stop it, now," said Nora laughingly, as she pushed away his hands.   "I thought you were anxious to meet the guys.   Let's get going."

The Lite House was a typical sandwich shop, not meant for anything other than a place to get good food and hang out with friends. True to its name, it was decorated with miniature lighthouses, which were copies of those found around the mitten state.   There were also pictures of Lake Michigan and ships which were placed on the walls in a haphazard pattern.   The hostess stand, which was not being used because the "seat yourself" sign was turned toward the entrance, had a ship's wheel on the front.   As soon as Will and Nora entered, they heard someone call out to them.   There was a long table down the center of the dining area where several people were already seated. Will was laughing and calling out old nicknames from his childhood, as they each hugged and gave each other back slaps.   Nora stood by politely until Will was finished greeting his friends, then he suddenly turned as soon as he remembered Nora was there with him.

"Guys, this is my lovely wife, Nora.   Nora meet Ted Bennett, Chase Phillips, and Ben Anderson."

Nora looked intently at each man as she said hello.   She wanted to try to remember who was who.   Ted was quite a bit rounder than the others.   He had already begun a receding hairline, and sported a very friendly face.   Nora knew immediately she would like him.   Ben had a boyish face which echoed his shyness.   He forced a small smile, nodded, and then looked down at his menu.   Chase stood up and shook Nora's hand across the table.   He was tall, with blonde hair and deep brown eyes.   Nora thought his coloring was striking, and immediately sensed an attraction which was quite unsettling.   Chase's face showed open curiosity as he looked her right in the eye, and as he did so, Nora felt something intense go right through her.   It was very disturbing, and she wasn't sure she liked it.   She was flustered and didn't want Will to see, so she immediately pulled her hand back.

"Will, you old son-of-a-gun, how did you ever score such a beauty?"

"Luck, Chase, pure luck."

They went around the table telling each

other a little about their lives to fill Will in.   Ted owned the hardware store down the street, and Ben worked for him in the paint department. Ted's wife, Paige, owned the quilt shop called Fabrications.

"I'm sure I'll meet her soon, then," said Nora.   "I have to visit every quilt shop I pass, just to see if there are any new fabrics of interest. Will can get a little annoyed with me at times because of my passion."

Ted grinned and said, "I can't wait to tell Paige.   She'll be even more excited to meet you now.   She was stuck at the store today and couldn't get away.   I have those days, too, so beware if you plan to be a business owner; it can completely take over your life."

Ben, it seems, was married with two small children, but was currently going through a divorce.   Maybe that explained his quietness and the sadness in his eyes.   He had the look of a lonely, miserable man even though he was surrounded by his buddies.

Chase, on the other hand, seemed to be the lady's man about town. Still single and never married, and from Nora's point of view, he was probably living up to his name, *chasing* anything in a skirt, as the phrase went. No wonder she got such an odd feeling from him. The guys joked about his single status, and it was clear that they enjoyed living vicariously through his exploits.

"So," said Ted, "tell us. Are you sticking around? Buying the old mansion? We sure would love to see you move here."

"We haven't really made a decision yet, but we're close." Will looked at Nora and winked.

'Oh great,' she thought, 'he's pouring on the charm now. I'm sunk.'

"Will, next time you come, call ahead, and we'll make plans to take the boat out. It's been a long time since we all went fishing together.

Maybe Paige and Nora can get to know each other -- and Laney, too, Ben, if things work out for you guys, that is." He glanced at Ben, who immediately diverted his eyes. Nora couldn't see his face well, but sensed that he was holding back tears.

They spent over an hour rehashing old times as Nora listened in. Occasionally, she caught Chase staring at her, but he would pull his eyes away quickly, pretending he was looking at something else. What was it with that man? Ted was the first to push away from the table. "I've got to get back to the store, guys. It was so nice to meet you, Nora, -- and Will, wonderful to see you again. I truly hope you make a decision to move here. It would be so much fun to have you back."

"I'd better get going, too," added Ben. "My boss isn't as forgiving as Ted's if my break goes too long." He laughed at his own joke, and Nora was glad that, at least for a few minutes, his spirits were lifted.

"Chase, don't you have somewhere to be?" inquired Nora.   As soon as she said it, she realized it sounded quite cold and condescending.   "I mean, you never really said what you do for a living."

"I run a landscaping business in the warmer months, and in the winter I plow.   I mostly work for golf courses in the summer, and cottage owners who need to keep their driveways plowed out in case they come up during the winter.   So, my hours are my own unless I have a demanding customer."

"Perfect," exclaimed Will.   "We'll probably need your services if we buy the old place.   I can't imagine trying to keep that long driveway cleared all by myself."

"I'd love to help out.   Give me a call." Chase handed him a business card, and said his goodbyes, but not before looking Nora straight in the eye once again.

"It was a pleasure to meet you, Nora," he said quietly.

"Same here."   Nora's voice cracked with her discomfort; she glanced at her husband, but it seemed Will hadn't notice a thing.

Chapter Five

On the drive back to Lima, the decision was made to buy the Taylor Mansion in Taylor Ridge.   They both knew a lot was riding on this major change in their lives, but they were in full agreement that they were ready to take the step for a different and, hopefully, better future.   As soon as they got home and unpacked, Will called Nancy and put in an offer for a number much lower than the asking price.   They also asked that as much furniture be included as possible. After waiting agonizing hours for a return call, they received the news that their offer was accepted, and the house would remain fully furnished.   They were in shock but also overjoyed.   Nora suddenly realized that this could be the most exciting thing that had ever happened to her, and she loved seeing that Will was happy beyond words.

They decided to tell his father immediately, and that was not a pleasant conversation, but Will had stood up to him, remaining fully in control of the conversation. His father had been generous in the end, giving him a severance pay because of his years of service, which would help them through the lean times while they were getting themselves established.   Nora gave her notice also, but there would be no extra pay for her except for the last paycheck which was in two weeks. Suddenly it was time to say their goodbyes. They notified the landlord, and went about the business of packing, and making multiple trips to the bank and the title company for the closing. Then, all of a sudden they were on their way, in an over-packed car, which Nora was driving, and with Will following closely behind in the driver's seat of a U-Haul.

Nora would never forget the moment they pulled in the driveway of the huge manse. The house took her breath away and propelled her back in time. She had had many dream-filled nights imagining life in that house in the 1850s and beyond. But the best thing was, when they came to a stop at the top of the driveway, they found Ted, Ben, and Chase waiting for them, holding welcoming signs and cheering. There were also two women, Nora assumed must be the wives, holding dishes of food. When they exited their vehicles, there were hugs all around. Paige and Laney immediately introduced themselves, and as soon as the door was unlocked, all three women walked into the mansion, heading straight for the kitchen to unburden their arms. The men began to open the back end of the truck to see how much work they had ahead of them. It was going to be a wonderful place to live; Nora just knew it. One look told her that Will was about to burst with joy.

"Would you girls like a tour before we get started with the food and unpacking?" asked Nora.

Both Paige and Laney burst out in giggles. "Listen to you," said Paige, "already acting like the lady of the house.   Did you forget that we were both born and raised in Taylor Ridge? I've been in this house more times than I can count."

"Yes, me too," said Laney.   "I used to be a housekeeper when I was a teenager."

"So was I," added Paige.   "A lot of girls applied here as soon as they turned sixteen.   It was a fun place to work for a while, until cleaning toilets and scrubbing pans got to be a real chore.   But most of the local girls were very thankful for a chance to work here.   There aren't many jobs for teens close by. You might need to think about hiring someone to help out, Nora, especially before a weekend or holiday rush."

"Yes, I've been thinking about that. It would take a big load off my hands to have someone do the routine cleaning. Do you know of anyone who might be available soon?"

"I'll put the word out," said Paige, "but it might be difficult because most of the kids already have their summer jobs lined up, and as soon as the weather warms up the teenagers have so many other activities going on that most of them aren't very dependable. I'll let you know if I hear of anyone."

The men had begun carrying boxes in and had already dropped several in the kitchen area. Nora had taken the time to pack according to rooms and had marked each box accordingly.

She had hoped it would make it easier to find things once the car and truck were completely unloaded. They all seemed to work well together, and the laughter and teasing was music to Nora's ears.

"Break time," called Paige.

Nora glanced at her cell phone to get the time. So far there was not a clock in sight. "You're right. We have to get some food in these men, if we expect them to work all day. I brought some sandwiches. I didn't realize you were both bringing a full meal. This is amazing." Nora had her head in the refrigerator, looking at the bowls and plates.

Laney started to get a few things out of her basket. "Let's eat your sandwiches now, Nora, and add my veggies and dip, along with the drinks. We can save the main course dishes for supper."

"Sounds like a plan. We can put things out while the men are cleaning up. The next question is, do we have any place to sit. There are boxes everywhere."

Paige glanced around. "You girls pull the food out, and I'll push around some boxes and wash off the table. I think we can manage here in the kitchen for now. Maybe for supper we can move to the dining room."

As they ate, the women had a chance to talk about themselves a little. Nora learned that Laney and Ben were giving it another try. She was not told what the problem had been, but she felt, at this particular stage in their relationship, it wasn't necessary for her to know.

Nora also discovered that Laney liked to sew and was a regular customer at Paige's store, but she was not interested in quilting. Once Paige and Nora began talking quilts, the conversation was non-stop about hand-quilting versus machine quilting, applique techniques, fat quarters, jelly rolls, and upcoming quilt shows in the area. Finally, Laney laughingly put a stop to all quilting talk complaining that she was being left out. She pouted like a girl, putting her lower lip out, and they all laughed so hard Nora had to wipe the tears from her eyes.

"Hey, keep it down, will ya'? We're talking fishing, here," teased Ted, with his mouth full of a sub sandwich.

"Okay, back to work," said Will. "After that comment, the women are going to chase us out of here with knives in their hands. Never interrupt a hen fest! Don't you know better?"

The men all stood up, stretched, and there were a few belches released. "Hey," said Paige, "you're in a fancy mansion now. Mind your manners! Now get out of here! I don't want to see you again until suppertime, unless you have a box in your hand marked cleaning supplies."

And so the day went. They worked and ate and worked and ate some more. With each hour that went on, they got to know each other a little bit better.   Bonds were created as memories were being made.

Finally, it was time to call it quits for the day after the larger pieces of furniture were hauled in.   Although there hadn't been much they had brought from the small apartment; they had decided to keep their own bed, loveseat, and TV, just to have a few familiar things around them.   Once those were in place and the bed was put together and made up for the night, they felt they had a good start on the unpacking. The rest could be tackled over the next few days as Nora and Will gave the place a thorough cleaning.   The others had jobs of their own to deal with tomorrow, so they were sent on their way.

Will looked at the guys, and said, "Thanks so much.   I don't know how we could have done this without you."

"And me neither, ladies.   You were amazing today," added Nora.

"We're just so pleased to have you in our little group.   We're going to be great friends forever, I can tell," said Paige.   "And please don't hesitate to call if you need anything."

Nora looked at her and Laney and couldn't help the welling of tears which were forming in her eyes.   Then everyone waved goodbye, and made promises to stop by again soon.

Chapter Six

The days passed by in a blur of activity. Will spent a lot of time outdoors with Chase cleaning up the yard.   They had decided that was the best course to take since the mansion had already been a working bed and breakfast, so they felt they should show an appearance of success, as soon as possible.   Nora had read that curb appeal was everything.   Apparently, people would sometimes drive by to check out a place before they requested a reservation.   The traffic down their road had picked up quite a bit, but it was most likely just curious locals coming by to see what was going on.

Chase had brought his mowing and

trimming equipment and with the two guys' hard work, it was really looking good. Chase made some suggestions on planting around the foundation of the house, such as burning bushes or sand cherry shrubs. He said the red color against the white house would be spectacular in the fall. They also cut a border garden along the edge of the driveway. It was just the right time in the season to get some annuals planted – it would be a little costly but worth it in the end, he said – that area would be perfect for a long row of colorful petunias, marigolds, or snapdragons. Maybe a little of all three. He thought they should get in some tulip and daffodil bulbs in the fall. He encouraged them to mix in perennials with the annuals so there would be a continuous display of color throughout the season. Nora was amazed at his knowledge of gardening. She had thought he was just a grass cutter, but he had explained that he was actually a Master Gardener, and had always had a love of plants and flowers, even as a child.   Strange, thought Nora.   Her idea of a man who liked to hunt and fish was not that of one who also liked plants.   She was learning all kinds of new things here about the men of Northern Michigan.

While the men were working outside, Nora had been cleaning everything in sight. She started with a good dusting of the furniture and wall hangings.   The picture frames were packed with a thick layer of what appeared to be very old dust.   Obviously, the previous owners had neglected that area of cleaning.   Each one had to come down off the wall, so she could do a proper job.   Most were pictures of people from the 1800s; they each had a brass nameplate with their name and dates.   Nora couldn't wait to find out who they were and how they were connected to the house.   The previous owners had not been the least bit interested in offering any history to the house.   It seemed as though once they were done with the bed and breakfast, they had wanted to make a clean break. Nora wondered if she and Will would feel the same way after many years of running their own business. Would they, too, be burned out and tired of the day-to-day activities?

There was plenty of space left on several bare walls that could hold some nice quilt wall hangings. When things settled down, Nora decided she would get back into quilting; she had not had time to devote to sewing in several years, and she was really looking forward to it. Will and Nora had discussed what they would do in the winter in the lean times. He said it would be time for them to devote to fussing over the interior of the house, fixing small things, and maybe redecorating, as well as a chance to take time out for themselves, because, as he had pointed out, if they were successful, the summers months would be a bear to keep up with, and they would need that time to recharge their batteries.

One day, Nora was hard at work mopping and polishing the floor in the entryway.   She had her back to the door, and when her wall phone rang in the kitchen, she turned to put down the mop she held in her hands.   She was so startled, that she dropped the mop with a loud clatter, because standing in the foyer was a young woman in some sort of period garb.

"Oh, I'm sorry, I didn't see you there. Did you just come in?"   The phone continued to jangle, and Nora felt like she really had to grab it.   What if it was their first customer?   She glanced back and forth from the woman to the other room.   "I --I'm sorry, can you hold on a moment?   I'll be right back with you."

The young woman, you could almost call a girl, had a sweet smile on her face, and seemed very serene in a shy kind of way.   Her hair was piled high on her head and her costume was a beautiful, mint green, silk dress with a standing, ruffled collar that accentuated her long neck. There was a large cameo at her throat.   It was obvious that her outfit had been modeled after dresses worn by the wealthy in the mid to late 1800s.   Nora had no choice-- she wanted to talk to this lovely young woman-- but she felt she had to run.   She breathlessly grabbed the phone, only to discover that it was Will's mother, calling to see how they were doing.   She quickly hung up, after explaining that she would call right back as soon as possible, then ran back out to the foyer, to see what the woman wanted. But when she got there, she saw that the woman/girl had already left.   Strange, thought Nora.   I wonder if she had been sent by Paige or Laney to apply for a job.   They both knew how much cleaning was involved here.   Maybe they had found someone who could help out temporarily or perhaps work as a permanent employee.

Later, during pillow talk, she was telling Will about it.   "Did you see anyone coming up the walk today and enter the house?"

Will looked surprised that she would ask that question since, so far, company had been at a minimum and limited to their small group of friends.   "No, we were in the back most of the day.   Why?   Was someone here?"

"Yes, and it was the strangest thing.   A young woman came in period costume – I'm pretty sure she was looking for a job and probably thought she would show me the full effect – but she disappeared before I had a chance to interview her."

"Why don't you check with Laney and Paige; maybe they sent her over."

"Yeah.   That's what I thought.   Oh well, it shows that the locals are supporting what we're doing here, anyway.   I'll call the girls in the morning and see what they can tell me about her.   Maybe I can get her number and call her back."

Time was flying by too quickly, complained Will.   There was still so much to do. They needed to get this business running soon in order to have some help with the mortgage payments.   At least, with Chase's help the grounds were beginning to shape up.   Will spent his days inside more now.   He painted walls and woodwork where necessary, and polished the wood staircase and bannister, sometimes using dental floss and air cans to get into the tiny grooved areas.   The house had a wonderful smell of fresh paint, wallpaper paste, and linseed and lemon oil.   Nora ordered fresh linens for the beds and thick towels for the bathrooms.   She had discovered a quaint little gift shop in town that carried the most amazing candles made from beeswax.   They had wonderful earthy scents that were bound to lend a relaxing atmosphere to the rooms.   She bought some silk flowers and wreaths of baby's breath and ribbons to place in various rooms until the gardens started to produce next spring; then she planned on using only fresh flowers. So far she and Will had been having so much fun.   He was happier than she had ever seen him.   All of the decorating was tapping into Nora's natural creative ability, and she was loving every minute.

"Nora."   Nora jumped and almost dropped the dainty teacup that she was placing in the china hutch.

"Oh, Will, you startled me."

"Sorry, about that.   I didn't mean to sneak up on you.   You were so lost in thought. I called your name several times."

"Really?   That's odd.   What is it?"

"Chase and I were talking about the good old days --"

"Again?   You guys.   Maybe you should stop living in the past and grow up," teased Nora.

"Okay, okay.   But anyway, we were thinking about taking his boat out to the big lake before we get busy and summer totally slips away from us.   Once we start booking guests, I might not be able to get away.   Chase and I thought maybe Ted and Ben could go with us. It's a great time for Coho fishing.   Is this Sunday okay?   No plans?"

"Plans?   Where would we go?   We've been attached to this house for a month, now.   I think it's a good idea for you to get some fun time in and just relax."

"Thanks, Nor, you're the best.   I'll work it out with the guys and get back to you.   Maybe you girls can spend some time together while we're gone."

"That would be nice.   I'd like that."

"Okay, I'll see what I can work out with

Paige and Laney."

Will planted a quick kiss on Nora's cheek, then out the door he went, in his usual flurry of motion. Nora sighed. Will never did anything slowly. He was always in a hurry. It had caused him to make many mistakes, but he usually was able to put things right. And it made her happy to see him in such a good mood. She sighed, then went back to her teacups.

Chapter Seven

Things were coming together nicely in the old manse.   And Nora suddenly realized that they would be ready to open to the public soon, but there was one big problem -- she still hadn't figured out the whole "breakfast" thing.   She knew she had been putting off looking for recipes, and that was not like her at all, but she was having trouble getting motivated.   Most likely it was because of her previous experiences in the kitchen.   She was okay with boiling potatoes, opening a can of vegetables, and even frying a hamburger or some eggs and bacon, but beyond that, most of the time her food was a disaster.   She was truly terrified of cooking and had never felt comfortable in the kitchen.   It probably stemmed from her perfectionist mother, who was on her for every little mistake when she was young.   Her mother, who now lived in a condo in Florida with her newest husband, number four to be exact, never gave her a break, or so it seemed to Nora at the time. Nora's mother, Marilyn, always said 'the way to a man's heart is through his stomach.'   She had explained to Nora that there were many times when a girl would need to know the art of cooking in order to get what she wanted. Heaven knows, she said, beauty fades quickly, but a man is always hungry.   So she decided when Nora was about ten to start the training, but being a young girl who was just getting her bearings and coordination together, Nora had dropped eggs on the floor, spilled milk, and generally just made a mess.   One time she left the cookies in the oven so long that the fan turned on automatically and the smoke alarm went off at the same time. The look on her mother's face said it all. Nora decided right then and there she didn't like to cook or bake. Even though her mother had apologized for being so stern, and had tried to explain to Nora that she was just a little girl and it would all come in time, Nora never believed her. In her mind, she had failed at being competent and creative in the kitchen like her mother.

But now there was no getting around it. She had to learn. Their future depended on it, and Will was counting on her to make it happen. She was a big girl now, she told herself, she could surely read a recipe and make it work. So Nora sat down at the laptop in the kitchen and began to search for recipes, specifically for breakfast. She never knew there were so many ways to make muffins. And everyone seemed to have a different way to boil an egg, for heaven's sake! After an hour of searching she slammed down the lid of her laptop, and her eyes filled with tears. "I don't think I can do this," she said out loud.

"What can't you do?"

Nora spun around and was shocked to see Chase standing there. "Oh, I'm sorry I startled you. I just came in for a glass of water. Is there something I can help you with? Got a computer problem?"

Nora quickly turned her back to him and wiped the tears from her eyes. Then she put on a weak smile, swiveled back around, and said laughingly, "I was just having a moment. I'm kind of embarrassed that you caught me. I'm just flustered with my search to find breakfast recipes that I can handle, and I guess I'm feeling a little insecure."

"I can understand that. I'm useless in the kitchen, but you know who can help? Paige," he said answering his own question. "She's a great cook. She could show you some tips and probably help find new recipes.   She was always fussing in the kitchen when we were kids."

"Oh, did you know her well, when you were growing up.?"

"I guess, you could say that," he said with a twinkle in his eyes.   "She's my little sister."

"Oh, I – I didn't know that.   One of the many things Will neglected to tell me.   He has a habit of leaving out important information." She rolled her eyes and laughed.   It was the first time she had felt at ease with Chase.   "I'll give her a call; I wanted to talk to her anyway about this Sunday when you guys go fishing.   By the way, Chase, I've been meaning to tell you what a great job you're doing with the yard.   It's really shaping up."

"Thanks, I'm glad you like it.   It's been a pleasure for me to work on this place.   I see you've fixed up the living quarters back here, off the kitchen.   Is it comfortable for the both of you?"

"It's sure a lot better than apartment living, so we have nothing to complain about, and using the kitchen help's living quarters makes sense.   This way we can be completely separated from the guests, and when no one is here, we'll heat or cool just this part of the house.   It's actually quite cozy.   The help in this household had it good."

He glanced around a bit and then stepped to the kitchen sink to get his water.   "I'd better head back outside.   I just have a little bit more to do around the pond, and then I was thinking of planting a few more white pines along the driveway, if that's okay."

"Whatever you think will look good, as long as you stay within the budget that you and Will worked out.   Right now, there's no income whatsoever, so I'm starting to get nervous."

"Then I'll get going, boss, and we'll get this show on the road real soon."   He placed his fingers to his forehead and gave her a salute. Then he went out as quietly as he had come in.

Nora had seen another side of Chase today. He was interested in her problems, and he had actually engaged in a real conversation, instead of just his normal teasing and joking with the guys. Most of all, he had not turned that upsetting stare on her that seemed to go deep into her soul. Renewed, she turned back to the computer for another go at the recipes. She'd get this yet.

Nora had notes spread all over the counter when Will came in an hour later; his hair was completely windblown, sticking out even more than usual, if that was possible. "Wow, it's getting gusty all of a sudden." He stomped his feet, making sure none of the freshly cut grass and bits of mud were stuck to his shoes. He had started to pay attention to that possibility after Nora had chewed him out for tracking all over her newly cleaned floors last week. "Hi, hon', what are you up to?" he said, giving her a kiss on the cheek.

"I've been trying to find some recipes all morning, and I'm so frustrated. I think I'll put this on hold until I talk to Paige. Hey, why didn't you ever mention that Paige was Chase's sister?"

"Oh, sorry, I thought I had. Yeah, we all used to run all over the neighborhood together. Paige was always trailing behind us guys, and feeling left out. I guess, we weren't always as nice to her as we should have been. Though, later, Paige and I were quite an item -- when we were nine," he winked.

"Where have you been for the last few hours? I had a little visit from Chase when he came in for some water, but he never mentioned you needing any."

"Oh, sorry, I should have told you, I left to

go to town.   Had to get my fishing license, and I picked up a few things at the hardware store while I was there.   I needed tackle, too.   Then I started talking to Ted and Ben, and time just slipped away."

"That's another thing that has to be remedied," said Nora, looking over her reading glasses.   "We need to stay in touch at all times. You never know when there will be a crisis with a guest that I can't handle on my own.   I have to be able to depend on you, Will.   Will you promise to always be there for me?   I know it's a little late to be asking this now, because we're all in this thing, but I have to hear it from you in your own words."

"Of course, Nora, I'll always be there for whatever you need.   I promise.   This was my idea in the first place, remember?   I won't let you down.   I know I haven't always been trustworthy when it comes to some things, but this time I really mean it."

"Okay, I'll count on you to stick to your word.   Now, hand me Paige's phone number, please.   It's on that tablet over there by your elbow.   I'm going to put it in my phone right now.   I'm pretty sure I'm going to need her more than I thought.   I'm lost, here.   I can't tell the difference between blending and mixing. And how many teaspoons are in a tablespoon, anyway?   Do you sift flour before measuring or after?   Ahhhhh!"   Nora pulled at her hair, and Will ducked out before he was required to answer any of those questions.

Nora had made contact with Paige, and it was agreed that she would come over for breakfast when the guys were fishing on Sunday morning.   Laney had to stay home with the kids, so it would be just the two of them.   Paige was coming armed with some recipes, so they planned to have a good, old-fashioned, cooking lesson, and Nora was looking forward to getting to know her new friend a little better. She was ready for a girl's day -- in fact she needed it. For over a month now, it had been nothing but men traipsing through the house with hammers and saws and tool belts, all the while discussing things like PVC pipe, elbow joints, blown-in insulation, dry wall, and reciprocating saws. It was time for some girl talk. Time for tea, candles, gossip, and giggles.

Later that evening over a light supper of grilled ham sandwiches, veggies, and cheese, Nora brought up something else to Will, something she had been turning over in her mind for a while, now.

"Will, Chase mentioned that we should either paint the sign out by the road or get a new one. I've been thinking -- I think it's time to establish ourselves as new owners and rename the place to our liking."

"You mean *your* liking?" he asked with a

grin.

"Well, probably, because I have a great idea. I know it's always been called the Taylor Mansion Bed & Breakfast, but that has no meaning for me, other than the historical significance. I've been thinking about our new friends, and the many new ones we are bound to make. How about "The Kindred Spirit Bed & Breakfast"?

"I'm not sure I get it." Will looked a little puzzled.

"A kindred spirit is someone you feel a really close connection to, sometimes the instant you meet. You know that feeling that you know someone already? It's as if you knew them before you ever met them. It can also refer to the past, as in being connected in a past life. A kindred spirit is someone who is so much like you that they know your soul, but different than a soul mate, which is usually a romantic connection."

"I guess.   It must be a female thing, because it doesn't mean all that much to me, but if it makes you happy, I say go for it.   It has a nice ring to it.   It was good that you brought this up now, because I was about to order business cards and stationery.   And we'll have to update our website anyway, so we can add a name change there.   'Introducing, the new and improved Bed & Breakfast – The Kindred Spirit!'" said Will opening his arms wide and sounding like a carnival barker.

"Thanks, I'm glad you approve, but let's don't take this circus on the road.   I'm looking for a little respect."

"Nora, you're getting way too serious about this thing.   Remember the fun we were going to have?"

"Yeah, but that was before I noticed our funds were depleting quicker than I thought they would.   We need to make a living, and soon!"

"Everything is going to be all right.   I

promise.   Now, I need to get back to my paint brushes before they dry out.   I want to be finished by seven; there's a game on tonight that I want to catch.   Great sandwich, by the way."

Nora sighed and put her head in her hands.   Time spent chatting with the guys, baseball games, fishing.   She was afraid she could feel Will slipping back into his old carefree habits, and that meant less attention to detail. And that meant more work on her part.   What had she been thinking?   Will was Will.

Chapter Eight

Nora had been sitting at the computer for too long.   Her back was aching and her eyes were beginning to blur.   She realized that she was not going to get anywhere with this recipe thing by herself, and it was best left for her cooking lesson with Paige.   Maybe Will was right, she had begun to get too serious about everything, but it was their livelihood and their life that was at stake.   In Will's view if it didn't work out, they could always find something else to do, as long as he wasn't an accountant again. That's not exactly the way he had first presented this idea to her.   They were both supposed to work very hard until they began to see a profit and the fruits of their labor.

She decided maybe she should take a stroll through the house and admire what they had accomplished so far.   Maybe that would make her feel better, because for the first few weeks, Will *had* worked very hard.   She ambled slowly from room to room until she found herself in the front parlor, her favorite room.   It would be the place the guests could congregate by the fire, maybe read a book or chat with each other.   Someone might even play the beautiful baby grand piano that had been left behind. Nora still couldn't believe the owners had included that in the sale.   She imagined it was because it was just too difficult to move, and most people didn't have room for this type of piano anymore, so selling it could take quite some time.   She was thrilled when the Realtor had told her it was staying.

Nora had always loved piano music. She'd had a few years of lessons, and even though she had shown some promise, she'd had to give up taking lessons. Her mother had recently married for the second time -- or was it the third – and the new stepfather didn't like hearing her practice. He said she hit too many bad notes, and it went right through him. Of course, her mother was more interested in pleasing her new man than standing up for her daughter, so the lessons stopped. Nora could still recognize some notes on the sheet music and could pick out, with one finger, one tune she had learned as a child. It was a classic by Chopin, one of the nocturnes, but she wasn't sure of the number – possibly Number Two – yes, that was it. It was Opus No. 9, Nocturne Number 2, in E Flat Major. She was surprised that that had come so easily to mind, but then Miss Mason, her teacher, had practically burned it into her brain by making her repeat it each time before she began to play.   She sat down in the great room and plunked out the beautiful melody.   The keys were real ivory; she could tell because they were slightly yellow and the grain was visible.   They felt smooth and cool to the touch.   There was something very satisfying about knowing that she still retained that piece in her memory, even though it was a watered-down version for a beginner.   She had never been able to execute the turn at the beginning. It was the note with the little squiggle at the top. She remembered she had to play the note first, then go up one, back to the main note, then down one, and back to the main note again. When her teacher had demonstrated the way it should be done, it was so light and beautiful. But whenever she had tried, it sounded clumsy, and the notes were not evenly spaced.   It was now painfully obvious that nothing had changed over the years.   She supposed it was something that required a lot of practice.

When she was finished, she stood and trailed her fingers along the wonderful walnut casing.   Nora had noticed that pianos like these aren't found in anyone's house anymore; they all seem to be a high-gloss black, or sometimes a stark white, but to Nora's way of thinking, wood grain was class all the way.   She made a mental note to come back tomorrow with a good quality furniture polish.   She would make the piano the focal point of the room.   Maybe she could find a large cupid and a vase of flowers to put on top of a beautiful lace shawl, which she would drape gracefully across the top, just like they used to do in the past.

As she rose to go, her eye caught the portrait of the woman on the wall, above the piano.   She had seen it many times before, but for some reason, she had not taken the time to study it.   Today the woman looked eerily familiar.   She was sitting in a parlor chair, with her straight back not touching the chair.   She was wearing a red velvet dress with a strand of long pearls at her throat that had been wrapped several times and yet they still cascaded down her breast. She looked to be in her early twenties or late teens; she had brown hair piled high on her head, and a regal look on her face. Nora was especially drawn to her eyes. There was a sadness there – or maybe it was loneliness. It seemed the painter of the portrait had decided to portray her exactly as she was feeling at that point in time. But who was she? Nora wondered.

It was then that her eyes fell on the small brass plate on the bottom of the gilt frame. She was a little too far away to read the dates of the small print because the piano was in the way and she didn't have her glasses with her, but she could make out the name -- Honor B. Taylor. It was clear she was a relative of the man who built the house, but how she was connected or how far down the family line she was, was not shown.

Maybe it would be fun to find out more about the history of this family, and then she could share it with her guests.   The previous owners had left nothing like that for them, so Nora resigned herself to start talking to the locals to see what they knew about the Taylor family. After taking a last, deep, look into the young woman's eyes, Nora felt a chill, all the way to her soul.   She knew this woman, or had met her at some time.   But how was that possible?   That's crazy.   She had died many years ago, maybe one hundred years ago, or even a hundred and fifty.   Nora felt the goose bumps raise on her arms.   She slowly left the room, feeling like she was walking away from something very important.   The research would have to wait, but she would find out soon enough.   They needed guests in these rooms first.   So for now, she had to stay on task.

Chapter Nine

It was Sunday morning when Nora's eyes flew open with the realization that she'd slept longer than she had planned. Will had left at 5:30 a.m. with a quick kiss on the forehead while she was still half asleep. The bed was so warm and soft, and she was so exhausted, that she dozed off again immediately. But now she had to fly! Paige would be here shortly so they could make breakfast together. There was no time for a shower now, but she should at least look presentable. She pulled on her jeans and grabbed a fresh tee shirt from her drawer, then did a quick face wash, brushed her teeth, and pulled her hair back in a ponytail. She decided make-up wasn't necessary. If they were to be friends, she might as well let Paige see her at her worst, although that always made her feel a little insecure. In truth, there was nothing about Nora to make anyone think she was anything other than perfect. She was, in fact, a very beautiful woman, even when her face was scrubbed clean of cosmetics.

Nora padded out to the kitchen in her bare feet, and was just beginning to put on the coffee, when the back doorbell rang. When she opened the door, there stood Paige, struggling with some books and a few bags of groceries. Her hair was also pulled up in a messy ponytail; she wore no make-up, and had on a pair of jeans, and a bright yellow sweatshirt, advertising the last 10k run she had participated in. "Grab these, will you, please?" she grunted, as she handed over some bags, while almost losing the books. After relieving herself of her burden, she was able to get a good look at Nora. "Oh,

I'm so glad you didn't dress up, either! My alarm didn't go off, so this is what you get."

Nora laughed with relief. Maybe she had found her kindred spirit already. "I had similar problems this morning. We're quite a pair!" She looked in the bags that Paige had been struggling with. "What did you bring with you?"

"I wasn't sure what you had in your cupboard, so I brought the ingredients we'll need for the first few things we'll be making. Oh, and there's a few kitchen tools and a pan in there, too, in case you're lacking in that area."

"Oh, I most certainly am. I don't have a clue what I'll need, other than a few measuring spoons, and some mixing bowls."

Paige grinned. "We're going to take it easy today. Of course, you should always look for easy-to-make recipes – but also for meals that look and taste fantastic. It's okay to let your guests think you slaved in the kitchen.

I've got some real time-savers, here.   Let's get started; I'm famished."   She began to pull everything out of the bags.   It looked like she had raided her own pantry, because there was a bag of opened flour and a jar of previously used nutmeg and a container with only 9 eggs in it. "Let's see what you have in your cupboard.   We should have discussed this before I came over." Paige opened the cupboards and refrigerator, pushing and shoving items around to see what was there.   She moved as if she were in her own kitchen; Nora noticed she was very much at ease going through someone else's stuff.   Then again, why shouldn't she be, thought Nora; she had helped put it all away in the first place.

Nora felt a little helpless so she started to fuss at the sink.   "Coffee or tea?"

"Let's stay with the B&B plan, and make some Earl Grey, if that's okay with you."

"My favorite."   Nora flashed her a smile over her shoulder.   "Of course, not all guests will be tea drinkers. I plan to get a quality organic coffee. Any suggestions?"

"Sorry, I can't help you with that. I'm a life-long tea drinker. I don't' know a thing about coffee. Ask Chase. He thinks he's a connoisseur."

"What do you have in mind for us to make today?"

"I'm going to teach you how to make sour cream blueberry muffins, for starters. Do you like blueberries?"

"Yes, they're my favorite. Mmm, sounds good. And a good choice for Michigan, especially in blueberry season."

"I agree," said Paige. "I read that, in the restaurant business, you should try to use whatever is in season to get the best prices. It's too early for blueberries, but you can substitute other fruits, like currents, or cranberries. And of course, don't scoff at frozen; they're as good as fresh, and they keep longer. My next question is, do you know the difference between a Quiche, a Strata, or a Frittata?"

"A whatta?"

Paige laughed. "I guess that answer said it all. A quiche is the French version of scrambled eggs in a pie crust. A Strata is actually nothing more than the American version of an egg casserole. It's nice because you can make it the night before and bake it in the morning. And a Frittata is Italian. It's just a quiche without a pie crust. I thought we'd try that today. I even brought my iron skillet from home. I didn't think you would have one – but boy, is that baby heavy!"

"Do you think I can handle that already? These recipes sound way beyond my ability."

"You've got to get past that thinking. It's just ingredients, clothed in fancy words. Just remember to start with the recipe that takes the longest to cook or bake and work on the other item while the first one is in the oven. Simple."

"For you, maybe," sighed Nora.

"It's going to be fine, you'll see."

Paige, it turned out, was an excellent teacher.   She was patient with Nora as she struggled to sift the flour, and measure accurately.   Sometimes, she took over, as Nora watched, but then she would turn over the spatula or beaters so she could try it herself. Through it all they discussed a lot of things about their jobs, their past, their families, and their childhood, getting to know each other better as they painted the pictures of various events in their lives.

And finally it was time to eat their first breakfast together.   "I can't believe I helped make this!   It's fabulous, and as good as a nice restaurant any day.   I think my guests will love this kind of meal.   It's so much better than the usual bacon and eggs, which they can have any day of the week.   Thanks so much. Paige!"

Paige grinned. They were really getting along well. It was as if she had known Nora all her life. "It was fun. And I have so many more recipes you can use. And as soon as you get your stride, you'll be finding them on your own, and I'll be coming to you for suggestions. But for now, if you're finished, I'm dying for a tour of the house. I haven't been inside since moving day."

"Really?" Nora raised her eyebrows in wonder. "Where has the time gone? Let's go, then; we can save the dishes for later."

"Fine by me, but let's at least put the leftovers away. I always feel better when that's done. And then lead on!" They laughed that easy laugh that usually only comes to those who have known each other for a very long time.

Nora took Paige into the dining room first through the swinging kitchen door. Paige gasped at the difference Nora had made in the room.   The hardwood floors were gleaming, and there was a lovely Oriental area rug under the table that had been left behind.   Nora had placed an ecru lace tablecloth on the old Duncan Pfeiff table, which was surrounded by chairs with their famous lyre back design.   She had placed a clear glass bowl filled with yellow and white chrysanthemums in the center of the tabletop, and around it she had set the table with antique china, each one in a different floral pattern, but instead of being overly busy, it was stunning.   The chandelier overhead sent out sparkling rays of glimmer over the walls, which were freshly painted a soft robin egg blue.   It was a refreshing, relaxing color that Nora hoped would be well-received by the male guests who were probably only there at their wives' suggestion or encouragement.   The overall effect was very elegant.

"Oh, Nora, this room is so beautiful," said Paige softly. "I had no idea you were such a talented decorator."

"Thank you. I love color and design. I think I agreed to the B&B just so I could decorate to my heart's content." laughed Nora. "The previous owner took all of the dishes and flatware with them, so I had to find something quick. I shopped online at eBay for these dishes, but someday I hope to have a matching service of Royal Albert Old Country Roses. Now, let's go into the parlor. I want to ask you about something."

Paige had seen this room many times before, but Nora had rearranged some furniture and added a few of her own antiques and collectibles. "That Ming vase is new. Was that yours before you came here?"

Nora whispered behind her hand, as if she were telling a secret. "Don't tell anyone. That came from Walmart. I thought I would use things that can be easily replaced in case a guest has an accident; then no one will get upset."

"Smart. What did you want to ask me?"

"Do you know anything about the people who originally lived here? Who built the house, that is?"

"A little, but not much. My mother used to tell me stories when I was young, but unfortunately I didn't pay much attention. Sadly, she passed away a few years ago. She had lots of stories about my grandparents and great-grandparents."

Nora looked at Paige with a shocked look on her face. "What are you saying? Are you related to the Taylors somehow?"

"Why yes, I thought you knew. Will knows."

Nora rolled her eyes and sighed. One more fact he had neglected to tell her about this town and its people. "Of course, he does," Nora said with a sigh.   "But then again he never thinks to tell me anything.   Just like I was never informed that Chase is your brother."   She shook her head thinking about that carefree, easy-going husband of hers.   "Okay, so tell me. Where do you fit in?"

"I'm not sure of the names in the progression, but the original Taylor is one of my great-grandfathers.   My mother's maiden name was Taylor, so it's a direct line back from there."

"Really?"   All of a sudden Nora had a revelation.   "Oh, my goodness, that means that it's the same for Chase!   He's been working the grounds of his own heritage all this time -- but he never said a word."

"No, he probably wouldn't.   He wouldn't want to take anything away from what you have accomplished so far.   But he did tell me that he is enjoying taking part in the restorations and upkeep.   Personally, I think he always wanted the house for himself, but without a wife or partner, it would have been impossible to do by himself."

"Well, that explains some of the strange looks I get sometimes."

Paige laughed. "He can get pretty intense, I know. But he's a real softy at heart. He gets on my nerves on occasion, but as a brother, you couldn't ask for more."

"So what do you know about this young woman in the painting over the piano? I have the strangest feeling that I should know her."

"I'm not sure," she said leaning in to read the brass nameplate. "I don't recognize the name. You could try asking Mr. Reed at the motel. He's been around here all of his life. He might know something about the past, and then of course, we do have a small museum. The curator is very nice. She might be able to tell you a few things, or set you in the right direction, at least."

"Yes," said Nora, excitedly. "That's a great idea. I would love to get some folklore to pass on to my guests, so they can have a feeling of the history of the place. I think it would make their stay more meaningful."

"Good idea. I'll ask some of my aunts and uncles and see what they have to say, too."

"Thanks. The more help I can get, the better. Now, I want you to see the widow's walk. How are your stair climbing legs?"

"I'm good. I'll count it as my exercise workout for the day." They laughed in sync once more, on the same pitch and with the same inflection as sisters often do, and proceeded to the second floor.

Chapter Ten

The girls went up the huge center staircase, stopping at the landing to look out the beveled glass which overlooked the back lawn. Paige was commenting on the improvements Chase had made in the landscaping, when she noticed a swan on the pond. "Oh, look, Nora, the swan is back."

"It's beautiful. Wait. What do you mean 'is back'?" Nora sucked in her breath at the miracle of having a swan in her own back yard.

"Well, it's well-known around here that a single swan has come to this pond for years. And, of course you must know that they most often pair for life; yet in this pond, for over a hundred and fifty years, folks have only seen one.   And the strange thing is that it can't possibly be the same bird."

"That is weird," said Nora.   "I wonder if there's something in the water that most birds don't like.   Maybe I should have the DNR check out my water source."

"That might be a good idea, before your guests try to wade in the water," she said with a chuckle.   "But I'm sure it's fine.   The guys used to sneak over here to fish when no one was residing here."

The girls moved on down the hall to an area above one of the bedroom doors.   "This is the awkward part.   I'd like to find a way to change it.   Step back, please."   Nora reached up and pulled on a rope that was attached to a square on hinges in the ceiling.   Then suddenly a staircase emerged and came down on a rail.

"Okay, here we go again; hang on to the side rail."   When they reached the top, they entered the lovely cupola, a little cluttered and dusty, but beautiful just the same.   The exterior widow's walk went all the way around, but Nora explained on their way up the stairs, that she didn't feel safe with it yet.   She would need an expert to check it out before she would step foot on it.

Nora reached the top first, then gave a hand up to Paige.   As Paige was wiping her hands on her pants, Nora explained that so far she had not had time to go through the boxes and sort things out.   "Everything is just as it was when we moved in.   I had the guys drop them in the middle of the floor until I could find time to arrange my space.   It was difficult for them getting the daybed up here, but they managed without an incident.   I almost called it off."

"Oh, but someday, you'll be glad of it. I take it this is going to be your sewing room?" asked Paige, as she walked around the small area.

"Well, that's the plan, but it has to take a back seat for now. There should be plenty of time for sewing and quilting when the snow flies and there are no guests to take care of."

"Oh, you'll be surprised. I think you'll have business even in the winter months. There's always snowmobiling, ice fishing, and people who just want to get away to do nothing."

"That's encouraging. So, what do you think? Is this going to be workable for my new quilting room? I was hoping for your expert opinion." Nora raised her eyebrows in anticipation of Paige's answer.

"I think it's going to be fabulous, as long as you can lower the shades when the sun is pouring in. You don't want to fade your fabrics. Maybe a nice cupboard for your scraps and fat quarters would work.   You could also use those large storage tubs for now – oh my, look at the time," said Paige as she glanced at her cell phone.   "I've got to go.   I want to be home when Ted gets home, in case he brings fish.   He sure can make a mess in the kitchen."

Nora laughed.   "I guess that's something I'll have to get used to.   Be careful going back down.   I usually go backwards, it's easier for me."

The girls chatted all the way back to the kitchen, and just when they were about to say goodbye, Nora remembered one thing she had wanted to ask Paige.   "I forgot to ask, but did you or Laney send over someone to apply for work?"

"No, I didn't.   Did she say I did?"

"Well, that's the thing.   She didn't say anything.   I left the girl standing in the foyer because I had to run for the phone, and when I came back she was gone.   It was weird, too, because she was wearing a period costume.   I thought she might be trying to impress me."

"Well, we do have an Old-Fashioned Days Festival in July, and some of the people dress up for that.   I suppose that's how she got the dress. But no, I didn't even know you were looking for help, yet."

"Yeah, I think I'm just about ready.   I'll need to train someone, and I can't wait until the last minute.   If you know of someone looking for work, or hear who she might have been, please let me know.   I just hope she doesn't think I was being rude, deserting her like that."

"Sure, I'll ask around, along with questions about my ancestors and get back to you."   They gave each other a quick hug goodbye.   "I sure enjoyed myself, today."

"Me, too.   And thanks so much for the cooking lesson.   I feel more confident already. Can we try one more session?"

"Of course.   It would be fun.   Let me know when you have free time."   Paige squeezed her hand.   "I'm so glad you guys moved here."   And she went out the door with a little wave.

Nora smiled to herself.   She felt much closer to Paige after today.   It was nice to have a friend, she thought, you'll never know when you need one.

Chapter Eleven

The guys were having a wonderful time. Chase had picked them up in the wee hours of the morning, and after all of their gear was loaded in his large black SUV, they began their day of fun in the sun on the Lake.

Will was as excited as when they were going fishing as kids with a pole slung casually over their shoulders and their tackle box in hand. "So, what's the plan, Chase? Where are we heading?"

Chase glanced over his shoulder to the back seat. "My boat is at a marina about 45 minutes away. From there we'll take the channel out to Lake Michigan. I almost decided not to go to the big lake because there's a storm coming in, but I checked the weather reports and the Coast Guard reports, and it looks like we don't have to worry about it reaching us until later this afternoon. It's moving slowly across Wisconsin now. We'll be long gone by the time it gets anywhere near us. So, let's go get some Coho, gentlemen!"

The drive to the marina was a pleasant one with typical male talk. Jokes, fishing stories, and talk of gears and motors were the main topics. Sooner than Will had expected they were pulling into Chase's designated parking space. They began the chore of unloading and hauling everything to the dock area.

Chase led the way to a beautiful 26-foot boat, decked out with downriggers and outriggers. As they stepped off of the dock onto the rocking, wet deck, Will glanced at the area housing the wheel and gages. Everything was totally up-to-date, including a GPS system, and a sonar fish finder.   Will realized that Chase had a much better setup here than he thought he would.   He took a deep breath of the fresh air coming in with the westerly breeze.   It carried with it a light, fishy smell that was not unpleasant, at all.   In fact, it was a scent that he had missed so much.   The feeling of being home filled him with nostalgia, and he felt tears prick the corners of his eyes.   He really loved it here, but he knew it was best if he didn't let the guys see his emotion, so he quickly turned his back and covered with another joke.

Chase clapped his hands together and said, "Okay, guys, let's get started.   But first I want to stress to you, that I am a very safety-conscious fisherman.   I won't tolerate any rough housing on my boat.   We'll all abide by the State and Coast Guard rules and regulations. Agreed?"

"Of course," said Ted.   "I wouldn't want it any other way."

"Good, then.   Here are the life vests.   I don't care if you think you are a good swimmer or not.   You *will* put one on, or we don't leave the dock."

"Man, I hate those things," said Will, "but I want to go fishing, so I'll go along with your request, Captain!"

"You do sound a little like a school teacher, there, Chase," added Ted.   "We've all been fishing before.   We know the rules."

"It never hurts to repeat them.   Sorry about the tone of voice.   Okay, then, off we go. Let's bring home some salmon!"

As Chase explained, while they were slowly going through the no-wake zone of the channel, he was planning on taking them north towards the Platte Bay where there was a State salmon fishery.   They could go all the way into the Bay if they wanted, but he said you could get some great catches right at the mouth.   They all agreed it was a good plan.

"Will, buckle up that vest.   It's not enough to just have your arms through it."

"Yes, sir!"   Will saluted.   He noticed the other guys tightening their straps, also. Guess he wasn't the only one who didn't like to be restrained.

Their trip followed the shoreline, and even though the sky was still clear, the water began to get a little choppy.   The boat bounced and heaved over the waves as they progressed northward.   Will had not been on a boat in Lake Michigan in years and was suddenly feeling the effects of some seasickness.   He didn't want the guys to know, thinking they would think less of him, so he covered with jokes and foolishness. He threw some bait at Ted and doused Ben with a spray of water from his water bottle.   The guys took it in good spirit, but occasionally Chase would have to remind them that they weren't kindergartners and they needed to calm down.   Will would turn his back and try to take in deep breaths of air to quell the nausea, and when no one was looking, he relaxed the straps on his life vest.   He didn't like the restriction across his abdomen.   Realizing too late he should have worn a motion sickness patch, he finally had to ask Chase if there was anything on board that could help.   Chase offered some Dramamine tablets which he always carried in his first aid kit.   After a few minutes, the pills began to help a little, and Will began to enjoy himself again, but the rocking and rolling of the boat continued.

"Tell you what, Will, I'll get closer to shore, and then you can just keep your eyes fixed on the beach.   Sometimes focusing on something stationary helps."

"Thanks, Chase, sorry to be such a baby."

"No problem, it's not something anyone can control.   You either get seasick or you don't. I really didn't expect the water to kick up like this so soon.   We'll get our fishing in, and then make a dash for home."

They finally arrived at what they considered to be a key location, so they set their lines and began to troll, driving slowly and leisurely through the water, hoping for that huge fish to hit on a line and thereby, creating a story they could tell their grandchildren someday. The day seemed perfect.   Queasy or not, Will was happier than he had ever been.

While the guys were having their break from work, Nora decided it was a perfect opportunity for her to relax, too.   She grabbed a couple of home decorating magazines, and a cool glass of iced tea.   She carried them into her parlor – she finally felt as if it *was* hers, after making her own personal mark on it.   She lit a fire, not because the room was cool, but just because she had always wanted to sit by a fire and read magazines at her leisure.   As a busy working girl this had always seemed to be a very decadent thing to do.   She kicked off her shoes and curled up on the sofa, throwing a beautiful hand-crocheted afghan over her lap.   Between the fire and soft yarn of the blanket, she was feeling quite cozy.   She snuggled in, and began to feel extremely comfortable and relaxed. Flipping through the glossy pages of the latest edition, she dog-eared some possibilities for changes she could make in the bedrooms.   But soon her eyes began to feel heavy, and she decided to slide down a little further and lay her head on the pillow.   As she did so, her gaze landed on the piano and the portrait hanging above it.   She wondered what life was like in the 1850s for the woman named Honor.   Did she love?   Was she loved?   Was life hard, or was it easier than most since she lived in a privileged household?   She probably had maids, or at least one, to attend to her, and there must have been a cook, because Will and Nora's quarters were off the kitchen where the help had probably slept.

Most likely, the kitchen help had it best, being so close to a stove in the winter.   The rest of the help would have been on the end of the hall on the second floor, where the rooms were small and simple.   The woodwork was pine there instead of the more desired hardwoods, and was lacking the intricate carvings seen on the lower level.   The floors were also pine, and seemed as if they had not had the same care and varnishing as the highly polished floors on the main floor.

Suddenly Nora became aware of soft piano music.   She hadn't realized her eyes were closed – she must have dozed off for a moment – had she?   She slowly peeked out through her eyelashes.   Her heart began to pound as she tried to focus on what she was seeing.   It couldn't possibly be – but it was.   The young woman from the portrait was playing the piano! Nora tried to sit up, but found her limbs would not move; she tried one arm and then a leg. Nothing.   She was paralyzed in place.   What was going on?   Panic began to set in, and then she heard the tune the woman was playing. Honor, -- yes she was positive that's who it was, was playing Chopin's Nocturne No.2, from Opus No. 9, the same piece that Nora had tried to play just the other day.   She played it beautifully; the turn Nora had struggled with was executed flawlessly, allowing the haunting melody to come through with so much feeling and love. She was obviously a very polished pianist. Nora began to relax a little, but was unsure of what was happening.   She was still unable to move, and that was very unsettling, but she wasn't afraid, at all.

Suddenly, Honor lowered her head, rested it on her arm on the piano, and began to sob.   Strange though, this time Nora could not hear a thing.   The weeping was silent.   She could just see Honor's shoulders heaving, and she could feel her pain intensely.   I don't understand, I don't understand, Nora screamed in her head.   Then as suddenly as it had begun, Nora opened her eyes.   Hadn't they already been open to begin with?   Well, of course they were!   I could see Honor.   It was real.   She slowly tried to move her arms and legs, and miraculously everything worked.   She sat up a little dazed and completely puzzled.   She must have been asleep, but how could that be?   She could see and hear Honor at the piano.   Had she experienced sleep paralysis?   She'd heard of people in the sleep state being 100 percent positive that they were awake when they were actually sleeping.   Nora sat there a few minutes, trying to gather her thoughts.   She wanted to remember every detail of what had just happened so she could tell Will.   Will!   What time was it, anyway?   He should be getting home pretty soon.   She glanced at the clock on the mantle.   My goodness, thought Nora, I've been in the parlor for hours.   Where had the time gone?

At some point during her nap, it had begun to rain.   And just as she became aware of the downpour, the wind started to slam heavy drops of water against the window panes.   She could hear the rumble of thunder far off in the distance.   It was sure to head this way soon, and it seemed as if it was going to be a doozy of a storm.   She was just wondering what was taking the guys so long, when suddenly the front doorbell rang.   That seemed odd since no one ever came to the front, yet.   Nora stood up slowly, smoothing out her hair and clothes. She had no idea what she looked like, but she'd better get the door regardless.   As soon as the door was opened, she had a sick feeling in her stomach.   There stood all of her friends.

"Hi guys, what's up?"   No one was smiling, -- in fact at least two had been crying. Nora did a quick count in her head, Ted, Ben, Chase, Laney, and Paige.   Where was Will?

"Will?   Will?   Where's Will?   What's wrong?   What happened?   Tell me, tell me right now!" she screamed.

"Nora," said Paige softly taking her by the arm.   "Let's go inside."

"No!" yelled Nora, yanking her arm away. "Where's Will?   Take me to him -- now!"

"Nora, honey," said Chase, "we can't. There's been a terrible boating accident.   I'm so terribly sorry."   And then he too began to cry, as he choked out the words, "Will's gone."

Nora stared at him, thinking this must be some kind of a sick joke.   "What do you mean, 'Will is gone'?"   What was he talking about? And then she looked him in the eyes and knew.

Nora heard someone scream as her knees buckled beneath her.   She saw Chase move quickly toward her, and then everything went black.

PART TWO

Chapter Twelve

Eight days later, Nora sat up in bed, trying to figure out where she was. And then everything that had happened came flooding back to her all over again. She remembered being carried to bed by Chase after her legs had buckled out from under her. He had laid her gently on the bed as she screamed for answers and cried uncontrollably. Her friends had not left her alone for a minute, as she begged them to tell the story over and over again. She needed to hear it many times to be sure there was nothing else that could be done. Chase was the one who told most of it. He apologized over and over, saying it had been his fault for taking them out when there were storm warnings. The other guys could barely bring themselves to look her in the eye.

Apparently, on their way back, the wind had picked up and the Lake had changed from its normal-sized waves to very choppy water. The storm had come in a lot quicker than had been predicted, as was often the case with weather over Lake Michigan. Will was experiencing severe seasickness by this time, and not even the Dramamine was helping. Chase had the throttle wide open in a mad dash for his marina, but a few minutes after leaving the Platte Bay area, the waves began getting dangerously large; the radar showed a fast-moving thunderstorm heading their way. While Will was hanging over the side vomiting, an exceptionally large wave hit the side of the boat. Chase saw it seconds before it struck them and yelled to hang on, but it was too late.

Ted was slammed to the deck, Ben slipped and hit his head on a tackle box and was completely knocked out for a few minutes, and Chase was left standing trying to hang on to the wheel.

As soon as they all regained their footing, they began checking to see if everyone was all right, and started to put things right again. It was then that they realized Will was gone. He had apparently been knocked overboard, maybe hit his head on the boat, and with the life jacket not fastened properly, he most probably had slipped right out of it in an unconscious state. They yelled and called and when they spotted his life vest floating in the water, a panicked Ben was going to jump in the water, but Chase held him down yelling that he would then risk losing his life, too. They put in a distress call to the Coast Guard immediately. As soon as their boat arrived, and their story was told, they were instructed to get off the water, because it was too dangerous for a boat of their size. The Coast

Guard would continue with the search and rescue on their own, and would let them know as soon as they found anything.

The days went by in a blur. Nora could not get out of bed. She had called her mother, but, unfortunately, she was out to sea on a cruise to the Bahamas. Will's parents had been told, and of course, they were beside themselves with grief. They had wanted to come right away, but Nora had explained that nothing could be done until they found Will's body -- then they would have to figure out the arrangements. She had never been very close with them anyway, so she had not expected any kind of sympathy and support, not like what she was getting from her friends right now, and frankly, she didn't really want to look in Will's father's eyes, knowing that he would be blaming Will for his own carelessness. Will's body was never found, and the Coast Guard had to give up the search. As was often the case, they said, because of the strong undertow, they might not find the body for months, and perhaps never.

Nora got up to go to the bathroom, weakly stumbling as she made her way. She heard low voices in the kitchen, the same soft mumble she had heard the whole time she had taken to her bed. She needed to see her friends and thank them for their kindnesses. She decided it was time to face the world – a world without Will in it. She reached for her toothbrush and took a good look at herself in the mirror. She saw a pasty pallor that did not resemble her usual coloring at all. The shine had gone out of her hair; it just hung limply on her shoulders. There were large dark circles under her eyes, and the usual golden feline color, was now nothing but a dull hazel. She dropped her clothes on the floor and climbed into the shower, turning on the water to a hot scorching blast. She scrubbed and scrubbed, hoping to feel something again, but the heat did not seem to faze her. Her nerve endings were dead – just like Will. Under the hot water, she began to think of her situation, and it was then that she realized she was in real trouble. Not only had she lost her husband, but she had also lost her business partner, in a new venture she knew nothing about. She was living in a new state far away from home, and her mother was in Florida. Fear hit her in the stomach, and she clutched at her gut and doubled over. Her legs gave out once again. Paige found her on the bottom of the stall sobbing, after realizing that the water had been running way too long. Her friend, her sweet, wonderful, new, best friend, wrapped her in a large towel and sat her on the bed as she dried her hair by rubbing and squeezing it into a smaller towel. Then she got a comb and began to try to put Nora together again. Nora sat mutely and allowed Paige to tend to her as if she were a child.   She felt nothing but a dull ache in her heart, and she was sure it would never go away.

Finally she found her voice.   "What am I going to do?   Paige, what will I do?   I have a mortgage.   I can't run this place by myself. We haven't even started yet, and I'm so inexperienced."

"Don't worry about that now," said Paige gently.   "When you're ready, we'll all get together and help you work out a plan.   There's no rush; you said Will had an insurance policy, right?   That will help a lot, and until the money comes in, we'll all pitch in and help you financially.   Whatever you need, we're all here for you."

Nora smiled at her weakly.   "What would I do without you guys?   How can I ever thank you?"

"You can't, because we won't let you. Now, let's go get some breakfast."

Heads turned quickly, and the chairs were pushed back, as Chase and Ted saw Nora come into the room. She realized they must have been sitting with her in shifts, and it was this group's duty today. They each came over to give her a hug. Chase kissed her on the forehead in a very gentle and brotherly way.

Nora looked at them one at a time, then lowered her eyes as they began to fill with tears. She willed herself to stop; there had been enough crying – for now anyway. "I don't know how I can ever thank you for all you've done for me. You have taken precious time out of your days because I was too weak to face what has happened and what is lying ahead."

"Don't ever say that again," said Paige. "We're here for you because we want to be, and that's that. Done."

"Well, thank you.   But I realized, while I was taking a shower, that I have to begin to sort things out.   It's been over a week now, and I have faced the reality that Will is gone.   I have a brand new mortgage and no income. Something needs to happen.   I think I'll have to put the house right back on the market and just take my loss."   She sank in a chair as the prospect of accomplishing all of that entailed; it overwhelmed her.

Chase leaned forward and took her hand. "I think it's too early to worry about the house right now.   We've sort of come up with a temporary solution, and we'd like to tell you about it when you're ready to listen."

She looked at them again.   They were amazing.   They had lost a friend, and the guys had gone through the same tragedy that took his life, and yet they were all working together to take care of her.   She gave them a weak smile; she owed them that at the very least.   "First, I'd like a cup of coffee, and then I'm ready to hear what you have to say."

"Good girl," said Ted.   He jumped up to pour her a cup, so eager to have something to do that could help ease her pain.   "Cream or sugar?"

"Black, please."   When she had wrapped her hands around the hot cup of coffee, she said, "Okay, tell me.   What's the plan?"

"Okay," said Paige softly, with so much concern in her voice that it was difficult for Nora to even look at her.   "First of all, we should start by telling you that we did not want to leave you alone in this big old house for a minute, well, ever since it – you know—happened."

"You can say it," said Nora.   "I have to get used to the idea.   I'll have to deal with Will's death for the rest of my life, but I'm sure I'm not the first widow this house has seen, and I won't be the last.   So I'm ready to do whatever has to be done.   Thank God, that Will, as carefree as he was, always insisted on a life insurance policy, even when we weren't sure how we were going to pay the premiums.   He said he wanted to make sure I would always be taken care of."   Nora put her face in her hands and sobbed again, but this time she was able to pull herself out of it a little quicker than on previous days.   "Sorry, go ahead."

Chase put his elbows on the table and looked down for a few minutes, then said, "I'm sure you weren't aware of how we managed the last week or so, because you never asked, and that's fine.   We totally understand.   So, I hope you don't mind, but we moved in.   Well, one of us at a time did, and sometimes Ted and Paige together, or sometimes it was Laney and Ben, when they could get a sitter that is."   He looked a little sheepish, then said, "We took over one of your bedrooms upstairs.   Someone's been here with you every night."

"Of course I don't mind. You guys are amazing. I truly don't deserve you all. You were Will's friends, not mine, and you have taken such good care of me. I really don't know what to say to all of this."

"Now, what did we say?" said Ted. "We'll hear none of that talk. That's final."

"All right," said Nora slowly. "That worked while I was in my fog, but what else is there? Do you have something else to say?"

Paige glanced at the guys, one a time, and then nervously looked at Nora. "I'm not sure how well you'll like this idea, but it was the best we could come up with. You know Ben and Laney have children and can't be uprooted."

"Of course, and I wouldn't want them to be."

"And Ted and I each have our own businesses that need attending to, and we have a house that needs maintenance, etc."

"Yes, of course, you do.   I would never ask you to give up your normal routine for me."

"Sooo, we thought -- "   Paige was having trouble spitting it out, so Chase jumped in.

"The thing is, I live in a small apartment above the hardware store.   I could easily move in with you – well, I mean in one of the bedrooms.   I'd be here to maintain the yard and plow the driveway this winter.   And there would always be a male presence in the house. I know it could be awkward, and you might worry about what the town people will say, but I think it could work."

Nora bit her lip.   Things were a little better with Chase than at first, but she still didn't feel like she knew him well.   On the other hand, as a bed and breakfast owner, she had already decided to let all kinds of strangers live in her house.   "It might not be a bad idea, but I would insist on letting you live here rent-free in exchange for any work you might do around the house."

"I would have a hard time with that," said Chase.   "I know you need an income, and I was thinking the rent would help you out.   I'm quiet, I don't have any pets, and I promise no loud parties."   He grinned.

"I guess it could work, for a while at least. But, once I sell out, you'd have to make other arrangements."

"We'll see about that.   I have more thoughts brewing, but we can take it one day at a time."

"Yes, that's all I can do at the moment. What do you think, Paige?   He's your brother. Can I trust him?"

"I'll vouch for him.   If he gets into trouble, he'll have to answer to me."   Paige giggled, as she punched him in the shoulder. They all laughed, even Nora, and then she remembered that she didn't deserve to be happy without Will.

Chase began to move in the next day. They all decided the sooner the better so the burden on the others would be eased. He was a man of few possessions, so it was just a matter of carrying in a few boxes and suitcases. Nora told him to use the bathroom at the end of the hall as his personal bathroom, since it was right next to his room. It might be awkward to go out into the hall each time he wanted to use it, but he was very agreeable with the idea. Chase said it wouldn't be a problem to knock a doorway in the bedroom wall so the bathroom could be accessed from inside the room. It would be one of the first projects he would work on. It turned out that he was a man of many talents; home renovating was a hobby, and he said it would be a treat for him to work on the mansion.

Nora found comfort in her magazines, flipping through the pages, even though she sometimes didn't even notice the pictures. It was something she had always done before, and the routine of it seemed natural. She was struggling to find something normal these days. She also began downloading cookbooks on her e-reader, and had been leisurely browsing through recipes for breakfast meals. It seemed to take her mind off of her problems for a time. Reading cookbooks, she discovered, could be very therapeutic. She came across a baked French toast recipe that didn't look difficult at all. As she read she noticed that she could put it together the night before, and let it soak in the refrigerator overnight. She suddenly had to try it *now*; she needed to see if she was cut out for this bed and breakfast thing once and for all. If not, she would have to sell out for sure. No one wanted to come to a bed and breakfast that served lousy meals!

Nora gathered all of the ingredients and followed the recipe to the letter before she went to bed. She could hardly wait to get up in the morning to put it in the oven. She hoped Chase would be around to sample it, because she would need a second opinion. She was up bright and early in the morning; finally, there was a reason to get out of bed. The brown sugar and cinnamon mixture, with the sliced apples, produced a very homey smell as it baked, filling the kitchen with its aroma. It wasn't long before Chase came downstairs to see what was cooking. He wore a fresh pair of jeans and a black tee shirt with the logo of his company on it in white lettering. His hair was neatly combed, and he was freshly shaven. Nora was not used to seeing a man who was never rumpled. "What's for breakfast?"

"I'm trying a new recipe for baked French toast.   Want to be my guinea pig?"

"Okay, since you were trained by Paige, I guess I can trust there will be no food poisoning involved, so yes, I'd love to try it.   It's good to see you up so early this morning."

Nora smiled weakly and said, "I couldn't sleep, so I've been flipping through recipe books. I still have a fear of the kitchen, but as I was putting this recipe together last night, I almost – almost – forgot about everything.   It seemed good, if it was only for a few minutes, because when I finally went back to bed and tried to close my eyes to sleep, it all came back."

"Well, that's something, anyway.   You know, you do have to start living again, even if it feels impossible at the moment.   And who knows, maybe cooking will become your saving grace."

"I have to admit, it is very calming."   She was interrupted with a ding.   "Oh, there's the bell on the oven.   Are you ready?   Let's see what it looks like." Nora pulled out the 9x13 pan of golden brown deliciousness.   It smelled like Thanksgiving and Christmas morning all rolled into one.   The brown sugar mixture had turned into a caramel syrup, and the bread had lightly browned – not burned as what Nora had come to expect of her cooking in the past. "Wow, look what I made.   Maybe I can cook."

"I'll reserve that judgment until I've tasted it," said Chase with a raised eyebrow. Nora put a hefty helping on a plate for him, then held her breath. Chase brought a fork to his lips, blew on it first, and then popped it in.   "Oh, this is good!   Really, really good."

"Wait!" said Nora as she jumped up and opened the fridge.   "I forgot about the whipped cream."

"Ah, perfect.   Mrs. Carter, I think you've done it."   As soon as the words, "Mrs." came out of his mouth, Chase knew he had taken her down that dark path again.   "I'm sorry, Nora, I was just trying to make light of it.   You seem to be a little different this morning."

Nora's eyes filled with tears.   "It's all right, Chase.   I'm always going to feel like Mrs. Carter.   But it did remind me that I have no business being happy – not without Will here." And she ran out of the room, leaving Chase feeling like the man who had 'opened mouth and inserted foot.'

He finished his breakfast in silence, trying to think what to do next, and then decided it was best to leave her alone.   She would have to work out some things on her own.   He cleaned up her kitchen, saving some French toast for her on a plate, and then he left a note on the table saying he had to go to the golf course for a lawn manicure.   He wouldn't be back until suppertime.

Chapter Thirteen

The warm days of summer were coming
to an end.   The evenings were cooler now as the
calendar inched its way toward Labor Day,
which would be the signal for all vacationers that
the season was over.   It seemed impossible that
so much time had passed since Will had
drowned in Lake Michigan, and still there was
no word from the Coast Guard or any of the
County Sherriff's Departments of finding his
body.   Nora had had to face the reality that it
might never be found.   As it was explained to
her by a kind police officer, sometimes a body
would sink and get snagged on something on the
bottom.   Lake Michigan is on average 279 feet

deep, the deepest part being 925 feet, making it very difficult for finding shipwreck and boating accident victims.   She finally had to acknowledge to herself that it might never happen, so she decided it was best to have a small memorial.   The problem was that they had very few friends here, and Will's parents were in Ohio.   She had discouraged her mother from coming from Florida, because things had been strained ever since she had married that last husband.   Nora had not even met him yet, but Nora had finally come to understand that who her mother married was her own business, and Nora had to stay out of it.   Even though there had been some comments that Nora didn't appreciate about their move to Michigan, she had put them all aside.   Her mother did whatever she wanted, and Nora's life was her own, also.   Will's parents had gone ahead and had a memorial for him in Lima, quite soon after his death, for his family and friends there, but at that time Nora was in no condition to travel and had not wanted to leave anyway in case the body was recovered.   None of the parents were giving much support about her staying here.   What did they expect, Nora wondered?   This was the life she had planned to build with Will.   There was nothing in Ohio for her anymore.   No, she was firmly planted now, even if she couldn't hold on to the bed and breakfast.   Her friends had seen her through the worst she could ever have imagined for herself, and she would never, ever forget that.

Yesterday, over lunch at The Lite House with her friends, Nora announced that she was finally ready to move forward with the B&B. She would need their advice as to how to proceed.   How could she get the word out that she was open for business?   Where could she advertise?   Did they think it was too late in the season for her to recover some losses? Everyone pitched in with ideas.   Since Chase,

Ted, and Paige were all business owners, they knew how to advertise locally. They agreed that the website would be instrumental in bringing in business from outside Taylor Ridge. Ben said he had a good working knowledge of websites, and he could help with that. Paige suggested putting fliers in the fabric shop because quilters often came for classes she offered and some liked to stay overnight at the motel rather than take the long drive home at night. Nora remembered Will talking about a bed and breakfast magazine. She thought she could check out rates for advertising in it nationally, but agreed that it would probably be cost-prohibitive. Then Chase suggested the Chamber of Commerce, and a local West Michigan magazine which featured places to visit. Maybe she could get an article written about The Kindred Spirit there, he said. He knew someone who knew the editor. He promised to look into it. And so it went, with plans and thoughts flying around the table. Paige asked them all to do a blanket email to everyone on their contact list suggesting they give the B&B a try.   Nora went home feeling very satisfied, and for the first time was eager to get started.   The driving force was the money, of course, but most of all she wanted to see Will's dreams through.

Today Nora had gotten up eager to prepare a yogurt fruit cup.   It seemed very simple to make, but she wanted to see if it tasted good, and if so, what fruits would work best. She was also ready to try her hand at drizzling chocolate over strawberries.   It might sound simple enough, but she knew there was a technique she needed to master for getting it to look like it came from a five-star restaurant. She had an idea to offer strawberries on a pretty plate in the room when the guests arrived.   She was hard at work when Chase came into the kitchen.

"Good morning.   What's for breakfast today?" he asked eagerly.   He had begun to look ahead to his mornings with Nora.   Her food was turning out to be something very special, or maybe it was the conversation.   He hadn't felt quite so lonely lately and no longer felt the need to hang out in the bar.

Nora spun around, surprised that he was there.   She had been so hard at work she had not heard him come in.   "Oh, hi.   This morning, I am offering to my guests a turkey sausage pig-in-a-blanket, a fruit yogurt granola compote, and chocolate drizzled strawberries on the side.   Also available is locally homemade, toasted, sourdough bread, with apple-butter spread, fresh from the farmer's market.   Sound good?"

"Wow, Nora.   It sounds fabulous. You've really come a long way.   Fill my plate, please."

"Well, I'll never tell how many dishes I went through before I felt confident enough to offer it to you.   But I'm feeling better about this all the time.   I really think I can do it now.   Of course, once there are more than one or two rooms filled, I'll need help.   I sure wish I could figure out how to get in touch with that girl who was here when we first moved in.   She was fresh-faced and seemed eager."

"Who was it?" asked Chase with his mouth full.

"Oh, someone who just showed up.   I never got her name.   I plan to ask around today.   Got a job this morning?"

"Yes, I'm starting on leaf blowing now. I've noticed some of the smaller trees are losing their leaves.   Not a lot, but just enough to make a mess.   It won't be long before we're in full-blown autumn.   We've got a long way to go to get to peak color, but time passes by so quickly, it'll be here before you know it.   Then when I

184

get back, I want to come up with some sort of check-in desk for you. You shouldn't have to walk your new patrons into the kitchen to sign in."

"I've thought of that, too. I think that's what they did here before, but it would seem to me, going into the kitchen, would ruin the effect and excitement upon first entering this beautiful place. And besides, I'd have to keep the kitchen in perfect order at all times. Anything you can come up with will be great."

"Well, I'd better get going," said Chase, wiping his mouth with a napkin. "You've got another winner there, Nora. I'll see you later this afternoon."

Nora had been standing at the sink with her back to Chase when he got up to go. She suddenly had an odd sensation and turned around just in time to see him boring holes in her back with that strange stare of his. She thought they were past whatever bothered him about her.   He had been acting like they were friends now.   That look was so unsettling. What did it mean?   Did Chase hold something against her for moving into his family's home? Had he been hiding his true feelings all along? She resolved not to let her guard down and take care of herself and her property.   She would have to watch him carefully.

Chase walked out the backdoor, in amazement at how well Nora was handling things now, but he felt that she might be hiding some of her grief from the rest of them, by trying to put on a brave face.   He wished he could protect her from her sorrow.   More and more he felt the need to comfort her.   He wasn't sure what was happening to him, and it was very unsettling.   He had to admit, their renter's agreement was going very well.   He actually liked living here, and knowing that his family had been the original owners of this place made him feel grounded, and connected to the past.

He felt a part of something bigger than himself. He knew he had to be careful not to get too attached, because the mansion didn't belong to him.   He was really just an outsider, looking in at his own family history.   In another time and with a different paycheck and lifestyle, he would have done everything in his power to make this place his own.   But he had not had the foresight to see what could be done with the mansion, and when it came up for sale, he was not financially prepared to make an offer.   For now, he was content to help Nora fulfill her dreams.   He would never let her know how guilty he felt about Will's death.   He wanted to do everything in his power to make her feel safe, because something was wrong – very wrong.   He felt it. Maybe someday he could find a way to help change the situation.

As soon as the kitchen was cleaned up, Nora decided it was time she went outside for a walk around the grounds. She had not really paid too much attention to the lawn and pond except through the windows. She was never much of an outdoor person, so it had not been enticing to her at the beginning, and then when Will died, she had lost all desire to go out. But today was a perfect day, with a mild, balmy temperature, and she knew there wouldn't be too many of them left, so she walked out wearing her flip-flops and a soft cotton sundress, with her coffee in hand. The gentle breeze moved her hair across her neck, giving her a sensation of being lightly touched. Was that Will's caress? She quickly spun around, but of course she knew no one would be there. It was just that sometimes she forgot he was gone.

The ground was still wet with the morning dew. It felt cool and refreshing on her feet as the grass came over the top of her

sandals.   As she walked towards the pond, she
noticed tiny toads hopping all over the yard.
They each seemed to be going in opposite
directions, crisscrossing each other, heading to
no particular place.   She had the feeling that it
was part of a game they were playing, as they
enjoyed the warmth of the morning sun, much
like she was doing herself.   The pond was very
still, creating a mirror image
of the horizon on its surface.   Cattails were
standing tall along one edge, the blooms already
bursting, as the fluffy tufts of cotton managed to
escape with the breeze, taking their seeds to
another place and starting the cycle of new
growth all over again.   Nora stood on the edge
of the water and studied the bottom, what she
could see of it, that is.   There was a clean, sandy
bottom where she was, allowing her to see all the
way down, inviting her to wade in, but a few feet
out from the shore, it began to get weedy and
murky.   It seemed that Chase must have

cleaned out an area so guests could wade without feeling the squishy sensation of soggy grass underfoot that turned most people off. How thoughtful, she mused.   She kicked off her shoes and walked in.   The water temperature was just right; it was at that point where you could barely tell the difference between the water and your own skin.

She stood there quietly for a few minutes, enjoying the sensation of the waves lapping at her ankles, and then noticed the lily pads on the opposite side from where she stood.   None of the water lilies where blooming today, but she thought they probably had earlier in the summer, and she most likely had been too distracted to see them.   She had missed so much during her mourning period, and she now realized that, just as the passing of the seasons, her life would move on.   The grass continued to grow, needing continuous cutting, flowers bloomed and then needed deadheading, and now the leaves would soon turn color and fall to the earth.   It was time for her to take part in the changes that were coming, also.   Will would want it for her.   She was sure of it.   In this perfect place today, which seemed like a little piece of Heaven, she felt it to her soul.

Nora was startled when she heard a splash; her eyes went to a ripple on the water. Had a fish jumped?   Then she noticed two, big, fat frogs sitting on top of the lily pads.   It must have been one of their buddies taking a dip.   So they really did that, balancing on top of a wide floating leaf?   Amazing.   She had always believed that was just in children's books, sketched out by an illustrator to make the story more interesting for big-eyed children who were wrapped up in story time.   She had so much to learn about nature and her own environment. Nora stood very still and watched as one frog quickly stuck out a long tongue and grabbed an insect flying by, that had been completely invisible to her eye.   It happened so fast, she almost missed it.   It was truly an enlightening morning.

Then Nora turned to the right and walked to one end of the pond where a small dock was stretching out into the water about nine or ten feet.   It was just long enough to tie up the paddle boat which was bobbing and bumping into the wooden post of the dock.   Maybe some night soon, when the sky was clear, she would come out here and paddle to the center, lean back, and watch the stars.   But with no one to talk to about it, what fun would that be?   Still she had to learn to appreciate this wonderful gift she had been given by God even if she only lived here for a short while.   She believed God had meant this pond area as a solace for her, a healing place, and she vowed to come out here every chance she got.

Next, Nora worked her way to the large, black, wrought iron gazebo.   It was placed on a concrete base which showed signs of having been repaired many times.   Little stripes of lighter colors of cement had filled in cracks to prevent water from seeping in, which might then have created further damage when the water froze causing the cement to crack open even more.   She took the two steps up to the floor level.   Either Chase or Will had freshly painted the wrought iron a shiny black.   Even though it now looked almost brand new, she knew it must have been here for many years.   She stepped inside and looked up at the high arched dome. The decorative filigree artwork was amazing, reminding her of what you would find on a pair of Eastern European gold earrings or maybe a ring from the early 1900s.   It must have taken many hours of first heating the steel in a forge to a high temperature and then bending and curling the individual pieces before the artist was satisfied with his curly-cue work.   At some point, in more modern times, someone had installed a ceiling fan with a light which was hanging from the highest point.   She looked around and saw that the switch was right next to one of the support poles.   She flipped it on, expecting it not to work, and was pleased to see that the fan instantly began to turn slowly, moving gracefully round and round counterclockwise in order to suck the hot air up and move the cooler air down.   A little hum from the motor was barely audible, but gave her a comforting feeling.   It reminded her of being a little girl when her mother would allow the fan to run all night in the summer when it was hot, lulling her while she slept.   One of the guys had carried out and cleaned the lawn furniture, which had been stored in the old greenhouse. She remembered Will saying that it was okay for now, but they would need new pieces at some point if they wanted to be a topnotch B&B. Comfortable outdoor seating for relaxation was a must, he had said.

Nora lowered herself down on the lounge. The outdoor cushions, were covered in a faded floral print, a mixtures of colors that had, over time, all blended together. She made a mental note to replace them right away. Perhaps that was something she could sew herself, saving some money. It might be time to set up her sewing room in the cupola. She wondered what her guests would experience by relaxing in the gazebo, and what kind of view they might have from this vantage point. Because of the openness, the circle shape of the gazebo, and the raised level of the concrete foundation, she was able to see completely over the whole yard.

Nora began to feel a release of some of her grief. She could feel Will here with her, looking over what was to be their dream, and she knew then that he would always be in her heart. But now she also totally understood that even though he had made plans for the B&B, he would never be able to share in the completion of those plans with her, and she was completely on her own.   All decisions were hers and hers alone.   It might be a burden, but today she chose to look at it as a new adventure in her life. She would make the best of what she had to work with, and from now on she intended to become the strong woman she knew she was capable of being.   She shed tears of grief and happiness at the same time, and when there was nothing left and her weeping was spent, she went limp.   It was as if she had shed her old skin, and she now felt as new and fresh as a baby.

Either because of her early morning risings or because she was finally giving in and accepting her status, her emotions had suddenly drained her strength.   It might have been the steady hum of the fan, lulling her into an exhausted state, but she suddenly felt a need to slide down further on the lounge.   She crossed her feet on the foot rest, getting into a more

comfortable position.   Her eyes seemed so
heavy.   She had been getting up way too early
lately.   She should sleep more, and she knew it.
She had tried to go to bed earlier than normal so
she could get more sleep, but then the darkness
would come, and along with it, thoughts of Will.
Often she'd had to leave a nightlight on.   Even
with Chase in the house, she felt unsettled.   It
was difficult to get used to being alone.   Even
now, she could hear Will's voice and see his
tousled hair, always sticking out at odd angles.
She thought she could hear him laugh and call
her name, but of course, it was all an illusion.

     The sun was filtered through the filigree,
and as the fluffy cumulus clouds moved slowly
over the sky, it caused the warm sun to create
patterns and designs which moved over her
body.   She almost felt like she was the one
moving, slowly riding in circles, as if she was on
a carousel with no music.   The effect was
magical.

Well, enough of this, she thought, she had things to do, so she must pull herself together and forge ahead.   She wanted to talk to Mr. Reed at the motel about sending guests her way when he was booked, and maybe ask some questions about the Taylors, so she forced herself to sit up.   It was just at that point that a huge shadow passed over, and she saw the swan lower himself gracefully to the water.   She was afraid to breathe, in case any movement or intake of her breath would chase him away.   He tucked his wings in close to his body and began to paddle soundlessly across the pond.   He held his neck in a graceful arch; his orange beak a sharp contrast to his beautiful white plumage. Nora thought she had never seen anything so beautiful in her entire life.

Then she blinked her eyes to clear her vision.   It couldn't be.   She hadn't heard anyone coming.   There at the edge of the pond, watching the swan float by, was a woman, and although she couldn't see her face well, she thought she was the same person who had come for a job right after they had moved in. She was once again dressed in the period costume. Well, no that wasn't accurate at all. This time she was wearing lawn white, and there was a bustle at her back. She held a parasol high over her head, as the women had done in the 1880s or 1890s, to prevent the sun from coloring their preferred pale faces. She stood, as before, with a very straight back, and Nora could see her chest and back rising and falling in quiet sobs. Then she raised her gloved hand to her face and brushed away the tears. She slowly turned and looked straight at Nora without saying a word; there was a sad emptiness in her eyes.

Nora lifted her hand in a small wave of greeting and called out a quiet hello. But the woman just looked at her with no recognition. It was then that Nora realized that even though this person was the woman she had seen in the foyer, she seemed older.   There were angles and planes to her face that had not been there before.   And when she turned once again toward the pond, and Nora got a good look at her profile, she knew with the beating of her heart, that it was the same woman in the painting above the piano.   The very woman she had heard *playing* the piano!   That was why the woman in the painting had seemed so familiar.   Nora sucked in air, because she felt her chest was constricting and preventing her from breathing.   She must have blocked out the image of the woman, Honor, playing the piano, because just as she had been questioning what she was seeing, the doorbell had rung and the horrible news that was delivered by her kind, loving friends had changed her life forever.

How could this be?   Nora's breath was coming in ragged gasps; this was impossible to comprehend.   She turned her body slightly to see if anyone else was in the yard, that might see the woman also, but no, she was alone.   And when she turned back to her, to Honor Taylor, she was gone.   Where could she have gone? How could she possibly be here?   She had lived here over 150 years ago.   Nora began to wonder if she was going crazy.   "That must be it," she said out loud.   "There has been so much turmoil in my life, and I haven't been getting enough sleep.   Maybe I was actually sleeping right here in the gazebo, and it was all a dream, like before."   It was then she saw the swan; he was real.   There he was, still gliding gracefully across the water.   But he must have sensed her presence, so he raised himself up with his huge wings, and with nothing more than the sound of moving air as the wings pushed down and lifted him up, he left Nora alone, feeling completely dazed.

Chapter Fourteen

Nora walked slowly back to the house, constantly looking over her shoulder in case she might see the woman again.   But there was no one there.   The pond was now extremely still without even the ripples the swan and frogs had made.   She knew one thing for sure; it had not been her imagination.   And she had not fallen asleep and dreamed the whole thing; she was sure of that.   She had seen Honor Taylor standing at the side of the pond.   Was there really such a thing as ghosts or apparitions? Should she tell someone what she had seen? Would Paige think she was crazy if she confided in her?   She knew she had no reason to fear whatever it was; she had not felt threatened, at all.

When Nora entered the house she went straight to the parlor to study the portrait again. Yes, she was positive now. It had been Honor. In the picture she was approximately 18 or 20 years old, slightly older than she had looked to be when she had first seen her standing in the foyer. On that day, she had seemed fresh and eager for whatever was about to come her way. No wonder Nora had not been able to find anyone who knew her. The artist had managed to portray sadness in the portrait, and when Honor was at the piano she had been crying just as she had been today. This morning, Nora was sure she had seen a vision of her at about 40 years of age, and she was weeping once again. Something tragic had happened to Honor Taylor, she was sure of it now, and Nora made up her mind to find out what! The next question was where to begin, and how to go about it without the townspeople thinking she needed to visit a psychiatrist.

Now more thoughts and questions were flooding her brain. Was this the reason Will and she had been able to purchase this mansion for the insanely low price that they had? Had the previous owners been only too glad to get away from their "visitor"? Is that the reason they went to Florida before selling out, leaving all of their furnishings behind? And if that was so, why had no one ever mentioned it before? Wouldn't Chase or Paige have heard stories of ghosts? There were way too many questions to answer for now. She would have to tread lightly, gathering a little information at a time, so as not to tip her hand. Once Nora began a project, she never backed down. Finding the history of this manse had now become her main interest, but there was another project that needed her immediate attention, and that was getting this B&B operational, or she wouldn't be able to stay here long enough for it to make a difference.

Nora had just grabbed her purse and was about to head out the door, when the phone rang – the B&B line.   She was startled, because her friends always called her cell now; she ran back and quickly picked it up.   "Hello.   Oh, I mean –ah, excuse me – This is The Kindred Spirit Bed and Breakfast.   How may I help you?"

"Hi," said the soft, melodious male voice on the other end.   "I recently heard about your place.   I went online to check you out, and I really like the setup there.   Do you have any rooms available soon?"

Nora was so shocked she hardly knew what to say.   For a moment she completely lost her tongue and started to stutter like a grade school kid afraid of giving the wrong answer to her teacher.   "Uh – uh – well -- sure, we can most certainly accommodate you.   What dates are you thinking about?"

"I'd like to come in two weeks for a Friday and Saturday night," he said.

"Sure, that's perfect, because we do require a two-night stay on the weekends.   Is this for two?" asked Nora trying her best to sound professional.   Luckily, her years dealing with customers at Fancy's had kicked in, and she was starting to feel more confident.

"Yes, for myself and my fiancée.   We're looking for a little alone time, to plan our wedding."   He chuckled, and Nora could almost feel the joy through the phone.   "She says it's difficult to pin me down on the details, and she needs to get me away from work and family for a little while."

"Perfect.   We can surely give you plenty of alone time, and make it a special visit besides. Can I have your name, please?

"My name is Conor McAuley, and my fiancée's name is Kate Lemanski."

"All right, thank you. Could you spell those last names, please?" After the blanks were all filled in in the reservation book, Nora said, "I'll put you down and if anything changes, please be sure to give me a 48-hour notice or your credit card will be charged a service fee. Well, then, it looks like we're all set."

As Nora was saying goodbye, she thought to ask, "Oh, by the way, how did you hear about The Kindred Spirit?"

"Oh, I received an email from my cousin, Paige Bennett. I guess, it must be someone you know. I thought it looked interesting, and then when I got the same email from my other cousin, Chase Phillips, I decided to point it out to Kate. We've both been looking for an excuse to leave town for a while. It was perfect timing."

Nora grinned broadly. Of course, her friends had been hard at work, while she was

207

chasing ghosts.   She'd better not mention that to her new guests!   She needed to go over her menu list for the breakfasts, and make sure every last detail of the room she had planned for them was perfect.   It was two weeks away, but there was a lot to get done for her very first customers.   She hoped, after a few times, this would become second nature and less planning would be needed.   Could she do it all by herself?   Only time would tell, and besides, she had no other choice.   She felt an excitement she had not experienced in months.   But now she'd better get going so she could visit with Mr. Reed at the motel.

        Nora got in her car, closed the door and turned the key.   She sat still for a moment as she thought through the last several months.   It seemed like yesterday she had arrived here with Will, full of doubt, but he had convinced her this is what they should do with their lives. Now she was left alone; where was he now with all of his upbeat, positive thinking? Sometimes he made her so angry! And then she realized it was useless to be angry at him now. Will was gone for good. She had to deal with the cards that were dealt her. She wiped those ever present tears, which were always lurking and ready to surface at the most in opportune times, away. She wouldn't allow them to flow now. She had business to take care of.

She had not driven around town much. Will had done the driving before, and then her friends had taken care of her so well, she had had no need to even go out. But the trip to the motel was easy and straight forward. The traffic, which was very light according to big city standards, seemed a little heavier than normal. She actually had to wait at a corner for three cars to pass! It must be the time of day. It was already getting close to lunchtime.

Nora pulled the car into the motel lot and walked to the office.   Upon opening the door, an old-fashioned bell jingled, startling the dozing Mr. Reed.   He wiped a little spittle from the corner of his mouth, and automatically smoothed down his hair, as he struggled to stand up.   "Hello, Mr. Reed.   I'm Nora Carter.   I'm not sure if you remember me, but my husband and I bought the Taylor mansion.   We stayed here the weekend that we were first looking at the house."

"I sure do remember you.   And of course, I heard about your husband's passing.   I'm so sorry.   He was a very nice young man."

Nora swallowed hard, forcing the tears to stay at bay; she had no intention of crying on a stranger's shoulder.   "Thank you, Mr. Reed. Yes, Will was wonderful, and I miss him a lot, but unfortunately he left me with a bed and breakfast to run."

"Yes, yes.   That must be hard."

"I was hoping you would remember our conversation about sending guests to each other when we are booked up.   I'm prepared to carry out that agreement, if you are."

"Of course, of course.   That works fine with me," said Mr. Reed.   "Anything we can do to help out a new business benefits all of us in town."

"Thank you.   I know that at first, you will be the one sending people my way.   But I promise you, when I get to the point of being completely booked, I will think of you right away.   I hope to make this an equal back-and-forth arrangement.   I thought if you had some business cards, I could put them on my 'places to visit' table where I'll have other brochures.   I brought some of my own cards along for you, also."

Nora handed him the cards.   Mr. Reed grinned broadly, wrinkles cracking his face like a broken mirror.   "That is very kind.   Thank you.

I see by these cards, here, that you have changed the name of the old place."

"Yes, we thought we needed to start fresh. Will had approved the name change just before he died.   It was my idea, but he went along with it.   Chase Phillips helped me with the paperwork with the County."

Mr. Reed, broke out in full laughter now. "That Chase, he's a good one.   He'll do anything for anyone in need.   But he sure was wild as a kid.   I made sure to keep my daughter far away from him, if you know what I mean."

"So you know the family, then?"

"Yeah, sure.   Everyone knows everyone here."

Nora hesitated just a moment, but then plunged ahead with what she realized had been the biggest reason for her visit today.   "I understand that Paige and Chase are related to the original Taylors who first built the mansion. Did you know the Taylors?   Well, not the ones

from the 1850s, but any of that family line?"
Nora held her breath, waiting for the answer.

"Sure, of course, I knew their mama well, and their aunt, and I also knew their grandparents."

"Mr. Reed, would you be able to tell me something about that family?   Anything.   I'm trying to put a little history of the house together for my guests.   I don't know where to start except with some of the older folks around here like yourself."

"Pull up a chair, missy.   There's nothing I like better than talking about the old times. But I can only go back a few generations."

"That would be a great start.   Thank you! Give me a moment, please, while I fish out a small tablet I carry in my purse.   I'm sure I won't be able to remember anything unless I write it down.   Okay, here it is."

"Where do you want to begin?" he asked, as he lowered himself to a seat in his small lobby.

"Well, I guess the easiest would be Chase and Paige and then work backwards as far as you can go."

"Okay, let's see.   Chase and Paige were raised on Adams Street.   Their mother was Cora Taylor, and their father was Robert Phillips.   I don't have any dates for you on marriage or anything, but I'm sure you can get those from the kids.   They were a real nice family.   But like I said, Chase grew up a holy terror, running around here on his bike at top speed.   And then when he got a driver's license – look out.   But that's not what you're really looking for, is it?   Let me get back on track. Cora's sister's name was Nancy.   She married a guy named Eric and moved to the Eagle Creek area.   I think they had two kids, too, if memory serves."

Nora looked up from her tablet. "Was one of them named Conor, by any chance?"

"Yeah, that's it. He used to come visit Chase and Paige with his sister. Sometimes they stayed a few days so the cousins could play. My daughter liked to join in with the girls, that's how I'm able to remember it, I guess. That was trouble, let me tell you. My wife tried to keep them all occupied with games and crafts."

"Okay, so Nancy and Cora were sisters," said Nora, "and their last name was Taylor. Do you know anything about the next generation back?"

"Sure, sure. Their mama and poppa was Edward Taylor and Alice Harrelson. I knew them well. We went to school together. I actually had a crush on Alice through most of my school years, but Ed won out. I didn't mind; it was a good match. They moved into the Taylor mansion when his parents died. Alice wasn't too fond of the idea, if I remember correctly, but

Ed wanted to make sure the house stayed in the family.   The girls were teenagers then, so they had a few years to live there at least.   Then when Ed passed away, at far too early an age, Alice knew she couldn't keep up the place by herself, and they had to sell out.   That's when it started to pass from one person to the next. Sometimes the house was empty for a long time; after all, who would want to own such a huge place?   We were in an energy crisis at the time and fuel was very expensive.   Then at some point, I'm not sure of the date, the last owners bought it and turned it into the bed and breakfast.   I never got to know them real well; they stayed to themselves quite a bit.   I guess they were busy keeping their business running, like most of us are.   It must have been quite a bit of work running that place.   So, missy, I hope you're up for it."

He took a breath in his narrative, and Nora used that as an excuse to say that she had to keep moving in order to complete her errands. She thanked him for all of his insight.   She planned to compare what she had learned with either Chase or Paige.   Now that she had a start, she was excited to get going on this family history.   She couldn't wait until she had worked her way back to Honor.

Her next stop was Fabrications, Paige's fabric and quilt shop.   Nora had been in it only once, and that was when they had first moved to town.   Will took her around to a few places so she could see where her new friends worked and lived.   The visit to the fabric store was very short, because Will's attention span was next to nil in there.   She remembered wishing she had left him in the car.   But it was strange how much time they had spent in the hardware store that Ted owned.   Will was completely ignorant of the fact that she was bored to death, and he talked and talked with the guys.   Anyway, that was Will, and she had loved him even with all of his faults.   Sometimes, she missed those faults terribly.   Now that she was alone, it was time to pay attention to Paige's store, and show some interest in her life instead of the other way around.   Paige had spent way too much time caring for her, and Nora was looking for a way to return the favor.   Maybe a visit to the store would give her some insight.

Nora parked her car right in front of the shop with the front of the car aiming at the large display windows.   How nice it was to live in a small town.   Back home, she would have had to park in a large lot, fighting for a spot, and then walk in the rain, sleet, or snow to get inside. On the way back to her car, she was usually carrying a large bag or two with her purchases. Lugging them across the lot was a real trial, as she protected her fabrics from the weather of the day.   Walking was enjoyable on perfect, spring days, but in the heat of summer, it was so blasted hot that the tar burned the soles off your shoes. She could see that she was going to enjoy parking so close to the storefronts.

Nora could see right off the bat that Paige had a real talent. The window displays were beautiful, inviting her to come in and discover what was offered inside. The quilts and crafts shown were bright and seasonal. As she opened the door, the traditional bell tinkled. A few heads turned to see who entered, but most of the women that were there were absorbed in choosing new fabrics. One lady held a fabric swatch up to a bolt in order to match a coordinating color. Another one struggled to carry three whole bolts around with her, roaming the aisles as if she were on a hunt for big game, moving slowly and quietly and never taking her eye off the prize.

For the first time, Nora was able to get a good feel for the shop. Standing in one place, she let her eyes travel around the large room. The organized colors almost took her breath away.   It was always like that when she went into a new quilt shop.   It must be the way children feel when they view the candy aisle at the grocery store, wanting it all and not knowing what to choose.   All around the outside walls of the room, standing on their ends and side by side, were bolts and bolts of beautiful cottons. They were arranged by colors that artfully blended from one hue to another.   It was like one gigantic color-wheel.   Nora had no choice but to let out a huge sigh.   For a quilter this was pure heaven.

Suddenly someone was speaking to her. "May I help you find something?"   Nora jumped and looked to her side.   She hadn't noticed anyone approaching; she had been that deep in thought about what she could do with all of these fabrics.   A very short woman in her fifties, with untouched greying hair, was standing next to her.   She had a pleasant face and a welcoming smile.

"Oh, I'm sorry," said Nora.   "Was I blocking the entrance?   I was just enjoying the view."

"Oh, not at all, my dear.   We quite often see that reaction when the ladies come here for their first time.   No one ever expects a fabric shop of this caliber in a town this size.   We are very lucky."

"Well, actually, it's not really my first time, but when I came here before, I guess I didn't really pay attention.   I'm a friend of Paige's.   My name is Nora Carter."

"Oh, of course, you're the one who bought the Taylor Mansion.   You're doing a beautiful job over there, by the way.   We like to drive by every now and then and check it out from the street."

"Well, thank you.   I was thinking of holding an open house soon; maybe you can get a chance to drop by then and see the interior." Nora had just then come up with that idea on the spot, but it seemed like a good one, judging by the woman's face.

"I would absolutely love that. We always have company from out of town, and I just don't have the room for them to stay at my house. I'm sure some of them would like to try a B&B. Oh, my, where are my manners? My name is Camille. I'm here most of the hours we're open, or so it seems sometimes."

"Nice to meet you, Camille. Is Paige available by any chance?"

Camille raised herself up on her toes and looked over the rows of material. "I don't see her behind the counter. I'll go check. Maybe she's in the back room."

"That would be nice, thank you" said Nora, "but don't bother her if she's busy."

"I'll be right back, dear."

While Nora was waiting, she continued her trip around the shop.   There were colorful quilt samples hanging from the ceiling with their patterns pinned on the corner, as an example of how they were made.   Along one wall, were rows of fabrics for special occasions, such as weddings and proms.   The silks and satins were begging to be touched, so Nora obliged by trailing her hands lightly as she walked.   An all glass counter held lace collars and premade appliques all ready to apply, along with exquisite cards of fancy beading.   She moved toward the back wall, and stood there studying all of the notions, as they were called in the sewing world – buttons, threads, seam binding, etc.   Hanging up on a peg board were the wonderful tools that all quilters felt were must-haves: rotary cutters and blades, cutting mats, plastic see-through rulers of all shapes and sizes, stencils, and of course the one no one could ever do without – the seam ripper.   It was a perfect store.   Nora was totally absorbed, and therefore she jumped when Paige touched her on the shoulder.

"What are you doing here?"   Paige gave her a big hug.   "I'm so sorry it took me so long. I was on the phone with a supplier.   Come back to my office and sit.   She led her back to a cramped little space with just enough room for a desk and two chairs.   Papers were piled everywhere.   "This is the worst part of my business.   I have to keep the door closed all the time, because I don't want anyone to know what my life is really like.   Utter chaos."   She laughed with that wonderful giggle of hers.

"I don't mean to keep you.   I was out doing errands, so I thought I would stop in."

Paige raised an eyebrow in surprise. "I'm so happy to see you getting out.   It's about time; really it is, Nora."

"Yes, I know.   Something happened today, and it made me realize that life has to go on, whether I like it or not."   Nora's eyes began to fill again, but she took a deep breath and willed away the tears.

"What happened? Something bad?"

"No, just something odd. I'll tell you about it sometime, but it made me think, and it was a nice day, so I went to visit Mr. Reed at the motel."

"Really? How did that go?"

"Oh, fine. He's a real peach. We decided to send guests to each other when we're booked. I also asked him a little about your family. I hope you don't mind." Nora looked down at her hands, now afraid that maybe she had overstepped her bounds. She didn't want her new best friend to think she was snooping into her business.

"Of course, not! Don't be silly. I'm just as curious about them now as you are. What did you learn?"

"Well, he could only take me back to your grandparents, Ed and Alice. Apparently, he had quite a crush on Alice before Ed asked her to marry him.   He also knew your mother and Aunt Nancy quite well.   But beyond that he had no other names for me.   I'm going to spend a little time on the computer doing research tonight, and then I think I'll have to visit the library or the courthouse.   I heard a lot of the records are public, especially where the house is concerned.   But look, I'd better let you get back to work.   I didn't mean to hold you up."

   "Not a problem.   Camille does a good job of covering the floor.   It was so nice to see you. I'm really glad you're getting out, Nora."   She gave her a big hug and walked her to the door.

   "Don't worry," said Nora, "I'll be back. I'm inspired now to set up my sewing room." On the drive back, Nora was thinking of all the ways she could go about her search to find out who Honor was.   It was overwhelming and all so foreign to her.   She might need the help of a genealogist.   But where she would find one was another matter.   And, how much was that going to cost?

Chapter Fifteen

Two weeks had passed since Nora had received the call for her first booking. Since then she had had others inquire about her rates and available dates. One couple had booked the weekend following Conor McAuley's and Kate's. Nora thought that had turned out just right. That way she could sort of practice on Chase's and Paige's cousin, although she would make sure that they never knew that was what she was doing. She planned to carefully observe everything about their visit, in case there was anything that might need improvement for the next time. She had also worked out a short questionnaire that she planned to ask them to fill out before they left.

Chase had come through with his promise to make a check-in stand.   Nora was quite impressed with his work.   It was well made and fit in with the décor very nicely.   It was at countertop height, with a thick wooden plank which had been coated in polyurethane.   It was just large enough to hold the sign-in book, a small laptop, and a landline phone, which would be available to the guests.   There were no phones or TVs in the rooms, allowing for the most romantic visit possible, but Nora knew the way people were plugged in these days, that some would be carrying their own laptops and they would be able to access the free Wi-Fi and watch movies that way.

Chase was excited to see his cousin Conor, but he had agreed with Nora that after the initial greetings, Chase would have to stay out of sight, or this romantic getaway weekend for two could turn into a trip down memory lane, leaving Kate out of the conversation completely.

They worked together to place the stand in the room on the east side of the house, and behind the staircase.   Nora had been told this room was used as the drawing room when the house was first built.   It was the place the men would retire to after dinner to enjoy a smoke and discuss politics out of hearing of the women who were too delicate for such things.   This room, with its dark wood paneling, was more appealing to men than the elegant dining room.   The deep red Oriental rug had been left and was still in beautiful condition.   Perfectly placed in the center of the rug, was a very ornate billiards table, covered in a dark green velvet, almost certain to please any man.   Nora had purchased a smoker's stand with a humidor from an antique shop, and although smoking was not allowed in her B&B, it gave a very masculine feel to this room.   The heavy leather chairs had also been left behind, but Nora had placed two stained-glass floor lamps next to them; they were reproductions she had found online.   She was very pleased with the way the green and gold colors reflected off the walls.   She tossed gold velvet pillows on the rich burgundy sofa. It was the perfect place for a guest to fill out the required paperwork and start their stay at The Kindred Spirit.   She took one last look around, ran her finger over a few surfaces to check for dust, and inhaled deeply to calm her nerves. The McAuleys would be arriving at any moment!

Nora ran up the stairs for one last look at the room she would place her first guests in.   It was one of the larger rooms and at the opposite end of the hall from Chase.   That should give them the most privacy possible.   It was also right next to the second bathroom.   This bathroom situation would have to be remedied one day soon.   Nora had thought of the possibility of sacrificing two rooms in the center of the hall to connect to the other bedrooms. She could create two bathrooms from each bedroom, thereby converting the manse to six bathrooms upstairs; that way each bedroom could adjoin a bathroom of its own from within.   It would take her eight bedroom inn down to six, one of which belonged to Chase, but she could get more money for each room that way.   And she didn't think she could handle eight bedrooms being full all at once anyway.   Especially by herself.   She would have to consult Chase on that idea.   Well, maybe she'd better call in a contractor for an estimate; she still wasn't sure of Chase's motivations.

She turned the doorknob slowly as if she were looking at the room for the very first time. Nora had given each one of her rooms a name of a flower or bird.   This room was called the Swan Room.   It was painted in a very soft shade of grey, with lots of white accessories.   The dark walnut sleigh bed was covered in a dusty plum satin comforter.   At the headboard there were four large fluffy pillows encased in white lace-edged pillowcases.   She had also casually tossed three, small, deep plum, throw pillows on top of the white pillows.   A silver tray was placed on the bedside table with foil wrapped dark chocolates, and a small bundle of dried lavender tied with a rose ribbon lay casually on the center of the bed.   There was a crystal vase with large white chrysanthemums on the dresser, and next to it, for a touch of color, sat a delicate, pink, Murano glass swan.   He was stretching his neck and airing out his feathers, and Nora was immediately reminded of the day at the pond when a swan much like this one was gliding aimlessly along while a stranger in a white dress and parasol looked on.

She hoped her guests would take the time to add to the journal she had left for their random thoughts.   She would ask each guest to write something about their experience here at The Kindred Spirit.   Her eyes scanned the room, and she inwardly felt a sense of pride with her decorating skills.   Yes, it was perfect.   Nora was pleased with her accomplishment, and she hoped they would be, too.   'Okay,' she thought, 'this is it.   They should be arriving any minute.'

She ran down the stairs and tried to catch her breath, as the almost unbearable wait began. She was like a small child waiting for the other children to show up for her birthday party. Finally, a car pulled up a full hour after their projected check-in time.   Nora had been on pins and needles, but they were here, at last. She smoothed her dress and prepared to answer the door.   She hoped to look casual and welcoming.   And she was sure she would, if she could just get her heart to stop beating so rapidly.

The couple got out of the car, both laughing at something. The man put his arm around the woman as they stopped to admire the beautiful architecture, before getting their luggage out of the trunk. Nora felt pride and excitement while she was looking out through the curtains, but she quickly backed away from the window when she realized they might catch her peeking at them. The couple walked slowly up the steps and rang the bell. Here it goes, thought Nora. She went to the door to greet them.

Nora opened the door to find one of the most beautiful couples she had ever seen and if two people were ever meant for each other, it was these two. The man had dark hair, and the most incredible blue eyes, so shocking that she had to catch herself from taking a step back. His smile was warm and infectious, and he immediately put Nora at ease. 'Wait,' she thought, 'shouldn't it be the other way around? Shouldn't she be the one to put her guests at ease?'

The woman was absolutely gorgeous; her shiny auburn hair swung sleek and straight at her shoulders.   She reminded Nora of a movie star from the forties, with her style and grace.

"Hello," said the man.   "I'm Conor McAuley.   We have reservations for this weekend.   I'm sorry we're late."   He smiled at the woman at his side in what seemed like a private joke.

Nora had finally gathered her composure, as she invited them in with what she hoped was a welcoming gesture.   "No problem.   This isn't quite like a hotel.   We want you to feel stress-free while you're staying with us.   Check-in times are just an estimate."

"Good, because it's all my fault, I'm afraid.   Hi, I'm Kate."

"Nice to meet you, Conor and Kate.   And you can call me Nora.   Please come in, and if you'll follow me to the drawing room, we can fill out the proper paperwork, and then I'll show you to your room."

"What a beautiful place!" Kate remarked. "I heard it was nice, but I certainly didn't expect anything this grand.   Look at the staircase, Conor."

"Yes, this is far more beautiful than Chase had described.   But then he was never a man of fancy words."

"You're right about that!" said Nora as she was writing the date and time on the form.   "I was surprised when you mentioned you are Paige's and Chase's cousin.   I absolutely love Paige.   She's my kindred spirit.   And Chase has been such a help; you know he lives here, right?"

"What?" said Conor, his eyebrows rising high on his forehead.   "I had no idea.   I was hoping we would get a chance to see each other. It's been quite a while.   Probably the last wedding or funeral."

"Well, we've both agreed that he will take time to visit with you for a short time, but this is your special weekend with Kate, and we want to keep it that way, so long talks into the night with your cousin are forbidden."   They all laughed with Nora's teasing.

"Thank you for that, Nora.   It's very difficult getting this man all to myself," said Kate, with a gentle pat on his arm.   It was clear by her look that they were deeply in love.

"Okay, if you'll sign here, we're all set. I've already run your credit card.   Aren't these little scanners for your smart phone wonderful? What will they think of next?   Here is your key. It's keyed for both your room and the front door, but you will not be able to enter the other bedrooms, and no other guest can enter yours. Nothing to worry about there, anyway.   You have the inn all to yourself this weekend.   Feel free to roam the grounds, explore, and use any room you like for relaxing.   The parlor is on the north side, and the sitting room is on the south; there's a pocket door for each room; feel free to close it for privacy, if you wish, since you're the only two here this weekend.   Through the sitting room you'll find the sunroom.   I serve breakfast in there on nice days.   If you need me after hours for any reason whatsoever, there's a bell in the kitchen which rings in my personal quarters.   Breakfast is served at eight, unless you prefer to sleep in a little, then I can easily adjust the time."

"Kate and I are both early risers, so that sounds perfect.   I'm usually famished in the morning."

"Great.   Would you prefer to eat in the formal dining room or the sunroom?"

Conor glanced at Kate.   "The sunroom sounds wonderful," she said.

"Perfect choice," said Nora.   "I'll walk you to your room, and then you're free to enjoy your weekend."

In the morning, Nora rose way before her guests so she could set the glass-top table in the sunroom.   It looked like a beautiful magazine cover.   She had placed a round bowl of pink roses in the center of the table, which was covered with a white linen cloth.   She had purchased the flowers at the florist yesterday, and even though they had been a little pricey, she wanted to make everything perfect for her first guests.   Maybe next year she would be able to cut flowers from her own garden.   There were two tall stands holding large Boston ferns, and near them an Oriental ceramic pot with a palm tree growing out of it.   The antique dishes and teapot made it appear as if the room was set in another era, just the effect Nora had been hoping to convey.   Kate and Conor had come downstairs right on time, and as soon as Nora was sure they were seated at the table, she arrived with a French press filled with hot coffee.

"Good morning," she said in her best cheery voice.   "I hope you had a pleasant sleep."

"It was wonderful," smiled Kate as she gave a quick sideways look at Conor.

"Hmm, yes, it *was* wonderful," he said with a wink.

Of course Nora realized that she was running a place that would be used for romance, so she would have to learn how not to intrude on private gestures and looks.   That seemed to be the case this morning, as Conor reached over to hold Kate's hand.   Nora suddenly felt a yearning for the romantic touches that she had been missing.   'No, stop, this isn't about me,' she told herself.   She must not cry.   "I wasn't sure if you wanted coffee or tea so I provided both.   There's a selection of teabags for you, caffeine, decaf, organic, herbal, etc.   I'm starting you off with some muffins, but I'll be back in a minute with your frittata and orange juice.   I'm sorry, but I neglected to ask if you have any dietary concerns, or if you are vegetarian or vegan."

"No," they both laughed.   "Kate does eat meat, but she says I'm the carnivore."

"Okay, good, then I'll leave you two alone, and I'll be back shortly.

The meal went exceptionally well, and Nora was pleased that she had been able to pull it off.   Nothing had burned or scorched, and she had actually received compliments on the frittata.   As Nora politely excused herself and went back to the kitchen, she loved hearing the happy chatter coming from the sunroom.

It turned out to be beautiful fall day -- warm but with the smell of fallen leaves and moisture in the air.   Conor and Kate decided to take a walk in the woods, and when they asked about what they might find, Nora was unable to answer.   She had not been out there herself since she and Will had first looked at the house. Maybe she had put it off because of the memories, but she decided she was ready now. She promised herself that as soon as her guests left, she would meander out through the path and walk back to the creek.

Two hours later, Kate and Conor returned.   They came in, laughing, through the back door, explaining that their boots were muddy, and they were sure Nora wouldn't want it tracked throughout the house.

"Kate, I love your red leather boots."

Kate glanced down at her hiking/work boots and grinned.   "Oh, thank you.   These were a gift to myself when I first moved to my log home along the Muskegon River.   I bought them online from L.L. Bean.   I thought they'd be great for walking the woods and working in the gardens. They were expensive, but I love them so much that it's been worth every penny."

"Everyone deserves to treat themselves once in a while, don't you think?" asked Nora. "Now, how about some hot chocolate by the fire in the parlor?"

"That sounds fabulous. What do you think, Conor?"

"Sure, I could go for that. My toes are cold. I wasn't wearing red boots." He laughed with a soft fuzzy chuckle.

"Okay then," said Nora. "You guys make yourselves comfortable, and I'll be right in."

When Nora entered with the hot chocolate on a tray, she saw Kate standing in front of the piano, studying the portrait of Honor. She turned and said, "I see there are portraits around the house of some of the Taylors, but this one is particularly beautiful and yet haunting. Is there a story behind it?"

"Funny you should ask," said Nora as she set the tray on the coffee table and passed out the steaming mugs.   She had actually jumped at her use of the word 'haunting.'   "I've just started to look into the family members who lived here, but I'm afraid I'm not very far.   I'm only back to your grandparents, Conor.   I'm really out of my element, here, and I don't know where to go next.   Do you have any information that would be helpful?"

"Not really, but you're asking the wrong person.   Kate, here, is a family research librarian, in other words a professional genealogist."

"Yes, I am," said Kate.   "I've been working on Conor's and Ellen's -- that's his sister, if you hadn't heard already – on their father's Irish family line, the McAuleys, but I'd love to take a detour and help out with Conor's mother's line.   It looks like the founder of this house was a very prominent person in the community.   It sounds like fun, to me."

"Really?   I don't know what to say.   I was just thinking I needed to hire a professional but, at this point, I know I can't afford it."

Kate laughed a delicate little giggle. "This will definitely be on the house, no pun intended.   After all, it's for Ellen and Conor, too."

Nora shook her head.   "What luck that you two came to stay at my B&B.   I can't think of anything I'd love to do more than to repay Paige and Chase for all of their kindness by giving them their family tree."

"I'll tell you what.   Since this weekend is just for Conor and me, as soon as I get back to Eagle Creek, I'll dig right in.   I don't think it will be difficult.   It sounds like all the Taylors stayed quite nearby, and maybe even continued to live here in this house.   I can email you or call with whatever I find.   I'm actually excited.   I love a new genealogy project!"

"Thank you, so much.   Oh, and by the way, Chase said to tell you, he'd like to see you when he gets back from work.   He promised not to take up too much of your time."

"No problem.   Maybe we can catch up while you girls get to know each other better," responded Conor.

"Okay, then," said Nora with her best hostess smile.   "I'm going to leave you two alone.   Sit in front of the fire as long as you want.   I'll be in the kitchen if you need me."

As soon as she had left the room, she heard Kate say, "She's very sweet, isn't she.   I feel so bad for her situation.   Please don't ever leave me alone like that, Conor."   Then there was a stillness as the two sealed their bargain. Nora once again felt her eyes leaking fresh tears. She brushed them away, lifted her chin, and went on with her day.

Chapter Sixteen

The McAuleys, or soon-to-be the McAuleys, went out for dinner later, and when they returned they were carrying shopping bags. It was obvious that they had found the local gift shops.   Nora greeted them to make sure all of their needs were taken care of.   She still wasn't quite sure when she should be present or when she should stay out of sight.

"It looks like you had a nice day.   I see a Fabrications bag there among the rest."

"Yes, it is," said Conor, with a chuckle. "I wanted to pop in to visit Paige.   Big mistake. The girls started in on quilting talk, and Kate ended up staying way too long, in my opinion."

"Oh, Conor.   She was helping me with colors and fabrics for the bridesmaids' dresses. It was so much fun.   And while I was there, I got an inspiration and Paige thought it was a good idea.   Conor did, too, so next we have to consult you."

"Me, why me?"   I was surprised to be included in their plans.   "Let's sit down, and we'll talk.   Do you want some coffee or tea?"

"Sure," said Kate.   "I'm excited to tell you what we have in mind.   Give us a minute to go upstairs and take off our coats, and I'll unload these bags.   We'll be right back.   Tea for me."

"I'm a coffee man," said Conor.   "I only drink tea to please Kate.   She forces me into it"

"Oh, Conor, that's not true."   And she gave him a playful slap.   "We'll be back in a minute."

"Meet me in the parlor."   Nora bustled off to the kitchen to get the hot water going.

She was glad she had brewed a fresh pot of coffee in anticipation of their return.

When everyone was settled in, Nora in the wing-back chair by the fire and Kate and Conor once again on the love seat, Nora poured Kate's tea. Kate began the conversation by saying, "You have such a lovely town, here. I really like Taylor Ridge. It's a wonderful little village. We took the time to walk the boardwalk through the dunes down to Lake Michigan. The scenery is beautiful, but, my, it's quite a hike."

"Yes, but we were able to make it with Kate's trusty red boots there to help. But seriously, Nora, this place is fabulous. We think Eagle Creek is special, too, but it's really quite different here. I think it's because it's wide open to the Lake."

Then Kate joined in by saying, "We absolutely love your mansion, and the grounds. The pond and gazebo are so romantic." She stopped a second, glanced at Conor, and said,

"We haven't been able to come up with a place for our wedding that suits us both, but we do agree that we don't want to take the formal route.   Paige and I came up with an idea, and I'm hoping you'll accommodate us."

"Accommodate you?" said Nora.   "I don't understand."

Conor joined in then.   "We'd like to know if we can hold our wedding here.   We had planned to get married in April or May, but we were thinking we could hold off a month or so. We'd love to be married in your backyard in June.   Hopefully, the weather would be more reliable then."

"A wedding?   But I don't know anything about handling weddings.   I'm barely into this bed and breakfast thing."

"But here's what Paige and I thought," said Kate.   "We can get a local wedding planner to work out all of the details, and I wouldn't even have to be here for any of it.   We'd communicate by phone, text, and email.   We're not talking about a big elaborate event, here. We'd pay you of course, for the use of the venue. And you would also have wedding party guests booking rooms, so that would be more income for you.   We're only an hour away, but I imagine some would want to stay over, and of course, so would Conor and I.   What do you think?"

Nora went into a panic at first at the thought of all of that responsibility, and then she took a deep breath and said, "Yes.   It sounds like a wonderful idea."   The minute it was out of her mouth, she thought 'what have I gotten myself into?'

Kate recognized the look of panic on Nora's face, having gone through similar feelings of distress herself, so she reached over to grab her hand and said, "I don't want you to worry about a thing.   The wedding planner will do it all.   All you'd have to do is take care of your guests the same way you would for any of your paying weekenders.   And besides, it's over 6 months away.   By then, you'll be a pro.   You have a real talent for this business, Nora.   We feel so comfortable here."

"Thank you, that means a lot.   It really is a good idea, when I think about it.   A wedding in the old Taylor mansion.   I'm sure there have been many over the years, and they were most likely Conor's family.   I like it.   Yes, let's do this."

Just then Chase came in the back door. Nora could hear him stomping as he tried to clear the mud and dust off of his boots, knowing he would face her wrath if he didn't.   "Just a minute.   I'll be right back," she said.

When she returned she had Chase in tow. "Conor, so glad to see you!"   The two men did a lot of backslapping and immediately started in with the teasing and jabbing.   Nora had never seen Chase so animated.   The women stood patiently by until the men suddenly realized they were not alone in the room.

"Oops," said Conor. "I almost forgot to introduce my lovely fiancée. Kate, this is Chase Phillips, Paige's brother. Chase, meet the lovely Kate Lemanski."

"Wow, Conor, how do you rate? She's beautiful!" They gave each other a hug, and Chase kissed her on the cheek.

As Kate stepped back, she teased, "I'm a little afraid to get too close. I've been previously informed of your reputation." She raise one eyebrow.

"Hey, Conor, no fair. Don't scare her off. I'm a changed man." He glanced at Nora to see how she was taking this information. Chase had recently decided that Nora's perception of who he was as a person was important to him, but she was grinning with the rest of them at this family jocularity.

"I have a plan," she said. "Kate, let's let these two boys go off by themselves for a few minutes." She looked at Chase and said, "And by that I mean exactly a few minutes." Then she glanced back at Kate to see if this was all right with her. A quick nod and smile assured her it was. "They can sit in the drawing room. You can join me in the kitchen if you'd like."

"I'd love that. Do you have a laptop available? Maybe we can get a start on the family tree. I have to look up at least one family member or I'll explode."

"Great idea. But I won't allow you to let this genealogy search take over your weekend plans. Agreed?"

"Agreed."

As the men settled into the large leather chairs, perfectly suited for their frames, Chase studied Conor intensely.

"There's that famous Chase stare. What's up, buddy?"

"Just looking you over for signs of trouble."   Then Chase laughed and said, "I see nothing but happiness in your future.   Truly, I mean it, Conor, I haven't seen you look this happy in years."

"Thanks, Chase.   I am happy.   Kate is the perfect woman for me.   You know, we actually met when we were only teens.   She was my first kiss."

Chase looked surprised.   "That's amazing.   How did you two get together again?"

"She moved into the log home next door to Dad's place.   I'm not sure if you remember the Lemanskis, but Kate's grandparents and mine both knew each other way back when. And through Kate's family search, we found out that we have a relative in common."

"Oh, oh, I see cross-eyed children on the horizon."

They both laughed. "It's too far back to worry about. I'll try to fill you in someday; it's rather confusing to me to this day. It's all on my McAuley side."

"You've got to watch those Irish," Chase teased again. "Seriously, I'm real happy for you. Hope I get invited to the wedding." He winked.

"Of course you will. As a matter of fact, Nora agreed to let us hold it here. So you won't have far to go. I know it's a little early to ask this, but I would love it if you were my best man. You've always been my best bud. What do you say?"

"I'd consider it an honor, Conor. I accept."

Then Conor said something surprising to Chase. "Now, what's up with Nora? How did it happen that you are living here?"

Chase looked down at his hands which were wrapped around his coffee cup. "Well, you heard about Will, right?   I'm sure you remember him from when we were kids."

"Yes, we did hear.   Paige told us all about it today.   Tragic.   That must have been awful for you, too."

"It something that I will never get over. And that's not the half of it.   Since his body has never been found, I think she is taking it extra hard.   I feel terribly guilty because it all happened on my boat."

Conor looked at him sympathetically. "You know it was an accident.   You must understand that deep down.   Nothing was your fault.   Don't beat yourself up."

"Of course, my brain knows that, but my heart won't accept it."

Then Conor grinned, and said, "But there's something else besides your living here to help out.   I see it in your eyes when you look at her.   You are very protective of her, and I think

I'm seeing tenderness and affection, maybe more.   Could it be love?"

Chase turned a deep shade of red.   He lowered his head, so he wouldn't have to look Conor in the eye.   When he looked up, his dark brown eyes had misted over.   "I've fallen hard, man.   I have to admit it.   She's wonderful. Strong, but fragile at the same time, and of course, as you can see, beautiful.   But she's still raw with Will's death.   I'll have to tread lightly if I'm ever to have a chance."

"Wow, this is serious.   Tread lightly? That's not the Chase I know.   I've never in my life seen you have a long term plan for a woman. I'm used to the love 'em and leave 'em kind of guy that you've always been."

"Yeah, I know.   It's not like me at all. But I kind of like the new grown-up version of myself."   They laughed together, and as soon as they realized they had been on sensitive subjects for too long, they veered into more comfortable male territory – sports.

"Here's the computer.　Do you think you can find anything that quick?"　Nora slid the laptop over the counter to where Kate was sitting.

"Oh, it's not always easy, but in this case with the people living in this house for so many generations, we have a good chance of finding quite a few of them."

"Here are the names I have discovered so far.　It's not much, because it only goes back to Conor's and Chase's grandparents."

"And that's exactly where we want to be. We always work backwards." said Kate as she logged into her ancestry site.　"This is good. Based on Conor's father's age, his parents were probably born in the twenties, so I should be able to find them living in their parents' homes in the 1930 census.   I'll concentrate on the Taylors, so I'll start with this Edward Taylor. He is Chase, Paige, Conor, and Ellen's grandfather.   I'll put in Edward Taylor, born approximately 1920 and place of birth – I'll guess Taylor Ridge, Michigan.   And boom, there it is!   Edward Taylor, born 1923, living with his parents, George and Frances Taylor.   It says George was born in Michigan, in 1899.   I'll jot this down for now, but I intend to create a new family tree, and then I'll save it to that account."

"Amazing.   I had no idea how to go about this.   I've seen the TV shows, but they always travel all over the world to get their information."

"I'm sure that's just for the viewing audience.   For some details you might want to go right to the source, but for the most part, everything is public information now and can be found at one site or another on the Internet."

Nora leaned on her elbows and looked at the screen. "I should be taking notes on this genealogy business."

"Let's move one step further with the Taylors. Now that we know George was born in 1899, let's go back in the census and look for him living with his family. We'll try the 1910 census, because at that time George would have been 11 years old. Again we start with his name, date of birth, and because we're not sure of place of birth, we'll put in place of residence as Taylor Ridge. And --- we have it. Just like that. He's living with his parents, and he's still here in Taylor Ridge. And if we look at the side of this document, we can see that this family is on Red Oak Lane. So they are still in this house. Wow! That's impressive."

"It certainly is. But it's just what I thought. They never left. So who are his parents?"

"George's parents are John E. Taylor, and wife Henrietta.   John is 35 years of age, so that puts his time of birth at 1875.   You realize that I'm just skimming through the male line.   We can go back later and check marriage and death records and city directories.   At that time we'll be able to get a more complete picture of their lives."

"Okay.   Can we go back further?"

Kate took a deep breath and let it out slowly.   "We've dodged a bullet, here.   John was born in 1875.   So we'll probably be able to find him in the 1880 census when he was five years old.   Most of the 1890 census, when he was 15 years old, was destroyed in a fire and there's nothing left for the state of Michigan, but if we can find him in 1880, we'll be good to go; otherwise, we'll have to go to birth or marriage records where his parents' names will be listed. Let's move on and give it a try.   Yep, there he is. A little boy living with his parents, John C.

Taylor, age 40 and his wife, Marissa, age 35. That's one more generation in the mansion!"

"Kate, you are amazing.   I would be so lost right now, without you."

"Well, there's room in their history here for one more census.   The 1850 was still good as far as family connections go.   Should we give it another try?"

"Yes, keep going.   I'm so excited."   Nora was about to come out of her skin as she realized how close she was coming to Honor, her ultimate goal.   Should she tell Kate about her sightings?   How would she handle something like that?   Perhaps it would be better to keep it to herself for a while.   She didn't want any of her new friends to think she was crazy.

"Okay, the next step is to input John C. Taylor, born about 1845, Taylor Ridge, Michigan -- 1850 census.   There he is at the top of the list. We'll click on that and there's the census record.

Nice.   I've never seen anything this easy in all of my years of doing family research."

"What does it show?" asked Nora leaning in again.

"Well, we now have John's parents listed as Charles Taylor, 44 years old, wife, Hannah, 34 years old.   And there's little John, with an 's' for son, and it says he's 5 years old.   Another son, Henry, 9 years old and, Sarah , who is 12."

Nora gasped.   "There she is!   It's Honor.   D for daughter?"   Kate nodded.   Age 14."   Nora ticked off the numbers on her fingers.   "So she was born about 1836. Amazing.   Kate, I'm shaking.   She was real. She lived here and played with her sisters and brothers here, and she most likely grew up and got married here."

"This has been so much fun," said Kate. "I never get tired of doing family research.   Let me make a nice list for you instead of my chicken-scratch.   Then you can see the proper order."

Kate took a fresh piece of paper, and she printed very neatly the names they had discovered so far.

Chase and Paige Phillips – parents, Robert Phillips and Cora Taylor

Conor and Ellen McAuley – parents, Eric McAuley and Nancy Taylor

Nancy and Cora Taylor – parents, Edward Taylor, 1923 and Alice Harrelson, b. 1924

Edward Taylor's parents – George Taylor, b. 1899, and Frances, b 1900

George Taylor's parents – John E. Taylor, b 1875 and Henrietta, b. 1880

John E. Taylor's parents – John C. Taylor, b. 1845, and Marissa b. 1850

John C. Taylor's parents – Charles Taylor, b. 1806 and Hannah b. 1816

"So I think we should stop there. George is the guys' great-grandfather. John E. is the great-great-grandfather, John C, is the 3rd great-grandfather, and Charles is the 4th great-grandfather, and by the dates most likely the original builder and owner of the mansion. Michigan became a state in 1837 and Honor was born in Michigan in 1836, so her parents were here as pioneers, and maybe were given a land grant to settle. We can find out more when we dig deeper. We'll also look into the women's maiden names which aren't given on the census records."

Nora quickly hugged Kate tightly. "This has meant so much to me. You just don't know."

Kate laughed. "I'm glad I could help. And I'll keep working on my end, but feel free to explore local history. You might be able to find out more at the library or the museum."

The men walked in to find the women embracing.   They both grinned.   "Looks like you two are getting along just fine," said Conor, pleased as punch, because if Chase had his way, and he usually did, Nora might someday become a permanent part of the Taylor family.

Chapter Seventeen

The next morning, Kate served one more breakfast for Kate and Conor. This time they decided to eat in the formal dining room, as it had turned out to be one of those gray days so common in Michigan. It had not begun to rain yet, but just didn't seem to be a sunroom kind of morning. This time Nora made the baked French toast that she had prepared the night before. She was so glad that she had practiced making this so many times, because it came out beautifully. The French toast was a big hit, and after a leisurely cup of coffee, Kate and Conor announced that they would be packing up to go. They promised to stay in touch with the wedding details, and Kate also said she would contact Nora as soon as she found out anything new on the Taylor family tree.

When they were gone, Nora felt a loss and emptiness. It had been so nice to have people coming and going to fill the days and take her mind off of Will's death. Sometimes, when she was busy in the kitchen or waiting on her guests' needs, for a few moments she forgot about the tragedy completely, but it wasn't long until that familiar ache came rushing back into her heart. When she was with Kate, Conor, and Chase, she almost felt part of a family, which was something that was missing in her life now. Maybe that was what she had needed, lots of people moving around in this big old house, to make her feel whole again. Perhaps some of the hurt was beginning to heal, just a little.

After Kate and Conor were gone, and Chase had left for his job at the golf course, Nora went about the business of stripping the bedding and cleaning the room that Kate and Conor had vacated. They had left it in perfect order, had even made the bed up again. She should remind her guests that it was not necessary on the last day no matter what your mother had taught you. She pulled off the comforter and tugged the sheets and pillowcases off the bed. Then her eye caught the journal which had been left on the bedside table. She wondered if they had taken the time to write anything down about their weekend, so she opened it to the first page, excited and nervous at the same time. The page was written in a beautiful script, very feminine looking. Kate had entered the date at the top and then began a short narrative of what they had done while they were here, then ended by saying:

My future husband and I were both completely satisfied with our stay here at The Kindred Spirit B&B. We were a little overwhelmed at the size and formality of the

Taylor mansion when we first arrived, but our hostess, Nora, made us feel like old friends. She was kind and caring, and seemed to have an uncanny sense for when we needed attention or when we preferred to be left alone.   The breakfasts were delicious and the setting romantic, including fresh flowers at the table and in the bedroom.   We thoroughly enjoyed our stay and plan to make The Kindred Spirit a regular stop whenever we need a little R&R. Thanks, Nora, for a perfect weekend.

How sweet, thought Nora.   My first review.   It felt good to know she had pleased them.   And she was sure she would remain friends with Kate, not only because of the wedding plans, but also because Kate was going to marry into the Taylor family, and would probably be close with Paige.

The bedding and towels were a little awkward to carry down the stairs. Nora decided next time she should remember to bring her laundry basket, and she must make a note that she should have a cupboard on the second floor that contained everything she needed for cleaning, including a second vacuum cleaner. Fewer trips would become a necessity when there were more people staying here.

When the room was cleaned to perfection and Nora felt satisfied, she decided to give herself a little break. After all there was no boss now to tell her when she could take one, so she had better get used to pacing herself. She was at the kitchen bar with a cup of tea and a magazine, when Chase came in. She was surprised to see him. "What brings you home so early?" As soon as it was out of her mouth, Nora realized that she had no business asking, and besides she had almost sounded like his wife.

But it didn't seem to bother Chase.   He smiled broadly at her, and said, "Haven't you looked out?   It's raining.   I can't get anything done with the leaves and grass when it's this wet out."

"Oh, no, I hadn't noticed.   I was cleaning and then decided to take a tea break.   Would you like some coffee or tea?"

"Sure, that would be nice."   He smiled at her again.   Nora had never noticed how perfectly straight and white his teeth were, an appealing contrast to his outdoor tan.   He ran his hand through his sun-bleached blond hair, but unlike Will's wild mop, Chase's fell right back into place.   How different the two men were.   And yet they had remained friends all these years.   Nora's eyes studied his body as he bent down to unlace his boots.   Long days of working hard outside had been good to him, honing and sculpting his muscles into a pleasing package.   Nora suddenly realized that she had been "checking out" a man, and she could feel herself blushing.   She quickly got up to pour his coffee.   "Black, did you say?"

"I didn't."

"Oh, well, I must be getting to know your habits, then."   She was flustered and she knew he saw it, so she covered by going to another subject.   "Chase, I have something I need to talk to you about."

"Okay," he said as he pulled out his chair. "Shoot."

"This is difficult for me to say, but I – I sometimes notice you looking at me in an odd way.   A stare that is very unsettling.   Is there something wrong?   I mean, uh, you've done it since the day I first met you at The Lite House. Are you upset that I moved in and took over your family mansion?   Because Will never told me that any of you guys had a connection to this place."

Chase seemed surprised and then embarrassed with her question. He wrapped his hands around his mug and looked down, a habit Nora had recently noticed. When he looked up, his eyes pierced right to her soul. "I'm sorry, I made you nervous. I didn't mean to. It's something I do sometimes, and if I tell you what it's about you might think I'm crazy."

"I doubt it," countered Nora. "Fill me in. Please. We need to be upfront about any problems if we're going to live together like this." If only he knew her little secret about Honor, then he would know what crazy really was.

"Okay, you're right. Only a few people in the world know about this, and Will was one. Conor is the other."

"Will?" Then it wasn't what she thought, or Will would have told her Chase didn't want them living there, wouldn't he?

"Yes, when we were kids, I confided to them one night when we all had a sleepover in our treehouse.   Maybe Will had forgotten because he moved away, and didn't see me experience it again, but Conor knows all about me."

"What in the world are you talking about?"

"Well, this is hard to say, but I see things, or feel them actually."

"What do you mean, 'you see things.'?" asked Nora.

"Unfortunately, I have the ability to see trouble that is coming to people.   Never happiness or joy, only trouble.   And the worst part is that I don't really know what the trouble is, but I feel it very strongly sometimes."

"What did you see when we first met?" asked Nora, intrigued, but almost afraid to hear the answer.

"I first saw one of the most beautiful women I had ever seen."   He grinned a huge Cheshire cat grin.   On another day and in another conversation he would flirt a little and perhaps forge ahead and tell her what he felt. But not now. "That might have been the initial look you saw, but I knew you were off limits. And then it came over me. I haven't felt it in a long, long time."

"What came over you? Spit it out, for Pete's sake."

"Nora, I felt grief. Grief so bad it kept me up at night. I knew you were going to have a rough time of it, but I couldn't say anything."

Nora jumped up from her seat, the chair crashing back. "You knew? You knew Will was going to die and you said nothing? How could you? You could have saved his life!"

Chase got up then, too. He tried to hold Nora's hands, but she pulled away. She pushed at his chest in what was intended to be a punch, but he backed away just in time, and she missed her mark. "This is exactly why I don't tell anyone. Please listen to me. I didn't know it was going to be Will.   I didn't even know it was a death, just deep sorrow.   If I knew, don't you think I would have stopped it?   I would never have taken him on the boat.   I'll regret that decision every day for the rest of my life."

Chased turned his back and placed his face in his hands.   Nora had already turned away from him.   Both were crying, Chase with a few gulps and then quiet tears, and Nora with full blown sobs.   They both stood their ground, and when their emotions were spent, Chase turned to Nora's back, and said, "I'm so sorry. So very, very, sorry.   I'd do anything to take away all of your pain.   I never meant to come into your world and destroy it."   He left Nora with her back still turned away from him, and walked slowly up the stairs to his room.

Chapter Eighteen

The days were flying by.   Nora and Chase
had not mentioned their emotional scene again;
both had chosen to ignore everything that was
said and act like it had never happened.   It
seemed the only way to proceed at that time.
Things had been awkward at first, but then
slowly, they moved back into their normal
routine of having breakfast together followed by
Chase leaving to do his yard work, while Nora
ran errands, took care of the house, and
prepared for guests.   Most often he didn't come
home in time for supper, so she left a plate for
him to heat in the microwave.

She'd had steady bookings since Kate and Conor had stayed at the B&B, and now Nora was feeling quite confident in her role as hostess. Usually, she only had one or two couples at a time, and she could handle that just fine.   The weekend after her first guests, a third cousin on Conor's side, named Audrey and her fiancé Gus had come for a weekend retreat.   Then shortly after that, Audrey's best friend, Melody, and her husband, Nick, decided they wanted to try out her place.   Conor's sister Ellen and her new husband Bart, booked a honeymoon weekend. It seemed that all branches of the Taylor family had been informed of her new B&B, and they were spreading the news to their friends.   The income was very nice, and with Chase still insisting on paying rent, she was now able to cover the bills without tapping into her own savings.   Chase was still taking care of the yard, saying that the work was payback for food, etc., but Nora didn't want that to go on too much longer.   She needed to have a talk with him, and she was dreading it.   Tension was still running high between them, and she had decided it was time for him to move on, even though she still really needed his rent money.

The leaves were turning color now that they were into the middle of October, and the day was glorious.   Nora thought it would be a good day to finally tackle the cupola.   One of these days someone would want to climb up there for the view, and she didn't want them to see her mess.   Boxes were stacked just as she had left them on moving day almost six months ago.   She grabbed a roll of paper towels and some window cleaner on her way up.   There were a lot of glass windows that were badly in need of some attention.

The climb was easy; she had been running up and down stairs for months now and was probably in the best shape of her life.   When she reached the top and emerged into the cupola, she was awestruck with the view. Even through dirty windows, it was spectacular. If nothing else the leaf colors of oranges and reds amongst the browns and greens would inspire any quilter -- but right now, it was time for work, Nora told herself. Relax and enjoy later. After a good cleaning of all of the glass, she began setting up her sewing table in the perfect spot, a place that would allow for light but would not cast a shadow on her work. She placed the machine she had purchased a few years ago at a thrift shop on top of it and set the chair in front of it. Nora tested out the chair to make sure the height was set at the right distance so her foot could reach the peddle, and then began the daunting task of going through her fabric stash. She sorted colors for hours – reds with reds, greens with greens, yellows with yellows etc. On moving day the men had carried up an old dresser for her, and she used that to hold her fat quarters and jelly rolls, smaller pieces that were cut from bolt ends and were meant to be used in appliqueing or piecing with small triangles and squares. She had a few larger pieces that had been cut to 2- and 3-yard lengths, so she neatly folded them and placed them in some large plastic tubs with lids she had purchased.

She had been sorting for a few hours, and her back was beginning to feel strained, so she stood and stretched and massaged her lower lumbar area. It was then that she suddenly had a feeling that she was not alone. There was no one in the cupola, so she did a full 360, scanning the yard all the way from the pond and to the woods and then around to the west side looking out to Lake Michigan. And there she was. Honor was outside on the widow's walk, looking out to the Lake with her hands to her brow as if to help her see farther. She had on a small fabric bonnet, one that would probably have been used to keep her hair neat and free from dust while she was cleaning. She wore a long apron, and the breeze gently moved the ties that hung from her waist.   Nora had never been this close to her except in the parlor when Honor had been at the piano crying.   At that time Nora was convinced it was a dream, but now she knew without a doubt this was no dream.   Honor stood perfectly still for quite a while with her back to Nora, when suddenly the cell phone rang.   She spun around to grab it to silence the ringer, and just that quickly, when she looked back, Honor was gone.

Nora waited for the beating of her heart to still, and then answered the call.   It was Kate.

"Hello?   Hello? Are you all right, Nora? Can you hear me?"

"Yes, yes I'm here.   I was in the middle of something, and it took me a while to position the phone to my ear," she lied.   "I'm sorry.   How are you Kate?"

"I'm fine," said Kate excitedly.   "I have some news for you about the Taylor family tree."

"Really?" said Nora. "I'm anxious to hear it. What did you find?"

"Well, I knew you were especially interested in Honor, so I decided to pursue that line, even though she's not a direct descendent of Conor's and Chase's, because remember, she's actually a sister to their 3rd great grandfather. I felt you, like I, had a special interest in her when we were studying her portrait."

"Yes, yes I do." How uncanny, thought Nora. What would she think if I told her I had been with Honor just seconds before she called? "Hold on a minute, I was upstairs, and I've been walking down to the kitchen. I'll want to jot a few things down, I'm sure. Give me a few seconds here to navigate the stairs -- okay go ahead; I'm in the kitchen now."

"Okay, but I'll email everything, too. Are you ready to write? You need to sit down for this."

"Yes, I'm ready.   I'm at the kitchen table now with tablet and pen in hand."

"I've been so busy at the library, but I finally decided I just had to sit down and work on this some more for you.   I thought the best course was to search for a marriage record for Honor, and I was blown away by what I discovered."

"Okay, okay, the suspense is killing me."

"The marriage record says that Honora Beatrice Taylor, married a William Cartwright on April 15, 1854, when she was 18 years old."

"What?   That's impossible!   I mean it's not impossible, obviously, but it's so crazy, I don't know what to say."

"Yes, I'm sure you're talking about the names.   I noticed right away, that Honor's full name is Honora –

--"which ends with n-o-r-a, Nora," interrupted Nora.   She could barely breathe. Honor's husband's name was William

Cartwright, and Nora's husband was also a William, known to all as Will Carter. "*And* I'm sure you noticed the similarity of the name of her husband, also."

"Yes, I was a little freaked out, I have to admit," admitted Kate.

"What you don't know, is that I married Will on April 15th, the very same day." Nora suddenly started to see stars and knew she was about to pass out. She tried to take deep breaths to slow her breathing down. What did all of this mean?

"Are you kidding? That's amazing. Well, I do have their death records, also. If you want to hear them, that is."

"Yes, please, go ahead."

"William died on Nov, 24, 1854 and Honor died in 1896, so she was 60 years of age by then."

Nora said quietly, "And Will died in 2014, not the same date, but 160 years later.   No wonder."

"No wonder what?" asked Kate.

"Noth—nothing.   It's a long story.   I'll tell you later.   Thanks so much, Kate.   Do you have anything else to shock me with?"   She tried a little laugh so Kate wouldn't know how shaken she was.

"No, that's it for now.   I'm still digging, though.   I want to continue with the patriarch, Charles.   I'll get back to you later when I have something.   I really should run; I'm on library time, here."

"Okay, thanks for calling.   I'll pass this on to Chase and Paige.   Talk soon, bye."

Now Nora knew why Honor was showing herself to her and no one else.   Or was she? Maybe she had been, and none of the others wanted to talk about it, either.   Was Honor trying to tell her something?   Or were her appearances something that had been going on for years?   It seemed like there would have been ghost stories if that were true.   Nora knew that she had to have a conversation with Chase about this, so all hard feelings would have to be set aside.

     Nora anxiously waited for Chase to come home.   She had prepared a light supper of sloppy Joes, her mother's baked beans, and seasoned baked French fries.   After seeing how he ate at the Lite House, she was sure it was something Chase would love.   Maybe she would even offer him a beer – better yet maybe she should have one herself along with him.   She might need some fortification in order to tell him what, or who, she had been seeing.

     It was well past seven when he walked in. Nora jumped up from the table where she had been patiently waiting, while swinging her foot and tapping her fingernails. "Hi, have you eaten yet? I made supper and I waited for you."

"Uh, no, I had a few beers with the guys, but we didn't eat." Then he laughed and said, "And drinking without food was not a good idea, if you know what I mean."

His speech seemed a little slurred. Nora decided on the spot that she had better forego offering him alcohol. "What's up?" He bent down to unlace his boots, lost his balance, then he looked up at Nora with a lopsided grin.

"What do you mean? I normally keep supper warm for you."

"Yeah, but it looks like there's a plate set for you, too. Are you eating with me tonight? Have you been missing my company?" And he actually winked, as he weaved slightly.

Nora was completely taken by surprise. He was flirting with her, and it looked like he had had more to drink than she originally thought.

"Well, I need to talk to you, but I think we'd better get some food in you first. You need to sober up a bit before you hear what I have to say."

Chase lurched forward, then threw his arms around her and placed his cheek next to hers, as he leaned on her heavily. "You smell so good. Oh, Nora, are you ready to start living again? Have you been lonely, too? Is that what you want to tell me? Do I have a chance with you? You'd make me so happy."

"Chase, what's come over you?" At first the feel of a man's arms around her and his masculine strength felt good, but then she came to her senses and pushed him away. "I've never given you any encouragement. Have I? I surely didn't mean to."

At that, Chase looked rather embarrassed and a little hurt, and he seemed to sober up instantly, or at least he pretended he had. "Forgive me Nora; it's the alcohol talking. I'll eat and then I'll be ready to hear what you have to say." Chase was convinced now more than ever that she was going to ask him to leave. He was sure he had ruined everything. They ate their meal in silence, then Nora asked him to follow her into the parlor.

Nora took the wingback chair with its back to the piano, so Chase would be forced to sit facing Honor's portrait. But first she asked Chase to start a fire; she would need the warmth and comfort of the flames to get through what she had to say. While Chase was squatting in front of the hearth, setting the kindling, he said, "I think I know what you're going to say. I should probably just save you the trouble and leave. I'll pack my things tomorrow morning."

Even though Nora had entertained the idea of asking Chase to move out, she was still shocked that he had sensed it. She covered by saying, "Whatever made you think that? No, that's not what I want to say, not at all. Please, just hear me out before you say anything. It's important that I talk uninterrupted, or I won't be able to get it all out."

"Okay," he said slowly. "Just give me a second to get the fire going, and then I'm all yours, baby." The moment he said that phrase, he could have kicked himself. It seemed he couldn't say or do anything right tonight. The coffee, food, and the simple act of building the fire had sobered him up, so he was now embarrassed by his earlier behavior. When he stood and turned to Nora, he avoided her eyes.

Once Nora saw that he was settled, she tried to begin, but at first no words would come. She ran her fingers through her warm brown hair, lifting it with one hand, then rubbed her neck with the other while slowly rolling her head back, not realizing that her motion was perceived as sensual to Chase. He didn't see someone relieving tension; he only saw the beautiful woman he had fallen in love with and was now certain he would never be able to have.

"All right, if you're ready, I have something to tell you, and when I'm done, you will most likely think I'm crazy. But first I want to ask one question. Have you ever heard stories about ghosts in this house?"

"Of course," said Chase. He was surprised by the question, but glad, at least, that they were finally talking. "When we were kids that's all anyone ever talked about. But then kids always think old abandoned houses are haunted. There was talk of seeing a woman on the widow's walk."

"Really? But no one you know has ever actually seen anything?"

"No, it's always been a big joke around here."

"Okay, here goes, then." Nora took a deep breath and began to tell him about her sightings.   She first told him about the young girl in the foyer she had thought was looking for a job.   Then about the day that Will had died, and she had actually seen Honor, the same woman in the portrait, playing the piano and crying.   She described how she could hear the music, and it was the same piece she had heard one other time.   Next, she told about seeing her at the edge of the pond watching the swan. "That time," she went on, "she seemed more mature; it was as if time had passed.   And the last time, I was in the cupola; she was on the widow's walk looking out at the Lake.   She seemed younger again that time.   I'm telling you, Chase, no matter what you think, it was real.   I felt no threat, just saw the visions." She stopped talking and realized that she had been looking deep into his beautiful brown eyes the whole time, searching for disbelief, but she saw no judgment there, and he seemed to take her seriously.   She was relieved that he was not going to make fun of her.   "So what do you think?   Do you believe me?"

"Of course, I believe you.   Why wouldn't I?   Look what kind of things I sense about people.   I don't understand that either, but it doesn't make it untrue.   I think you should investigate the story of Honor and the families who lived here."

"Actually, I already have a good start on that.   Kate has been helping me."

"Kate Lemanski, Conor's fiancée?   I didn't know you were still in touch with her."

"She's a professional genealogist and family history librarian.   She volunteered to help me with your family tree because it's also Conor's, but she doesn't know about the sightings.   I never told her that part.   There's more, if you can take it."

"Go ahead, I'm all ears."   Chase was actually more than happy to listen.   This way he could stare at her beautiful face all he wanted, and not have to steal furtive glances.   The firelight danced, making lovely shadows across her cheeks and highlights in her hair.   He could sit here and watch her forever.

"This part is really weird, and it freaked out both of us.   It turns out that Honor's full name is Honora.   Did you hear the last two syllables?   Nora.   *And* she married a William Cartwright, similar to Will Carter, on April 15, 1854.   I married Will on that exact same date, different year, of course."   Nora had been leaning towards the edge of her chair, and suddenly felt exhausted from telling Chase about everything.   She settled back into the large chair in a more comfortable position.

"This is unbelievable.   Well, not really unbelievable, more shocking really.   How does she fit into the Taylor family, then?"

"Kate has all of the documents that show that Honor was the daughter of Charles Taylor, the founder of the town and the man who built this mansion. She is your 3rd great-grandfather's sister. She lived here until the day she died. So what do you think? Am I crazy, psychic, or a little of both."

Chase thought carefully, before speaking. He didn't want to say the wrong thing. "I'm sure you're not crazy, and probably not psychic, because this has never happened to you before, has it?"

"No, never," said Nora, shaking her head adamantly.

""I've never heard of anyone seeing this Honor person, for sure. I'd say, she is coming to you for a reason. She has something to say, that's meant for you alone."

"Well, I can't think of what it would be. I only arrived this year, and have no connection to the family."

"I've had to come to grips with the feelings I get a long time ago. Once I accepted them, it was easier to take, except in my case, I can't do anything about it, and it usually means someone else is going to be in pain.   So that's not pleasant, at all.   But I think she wants you to rectify something she couldn't while she was still living.   You just have to figure out what it is.   She probably thinks of you as a kindred spirit."

Nora chewed on her lower lip for a moment as she remembered how she had suddenly, out of the blue, wanted to change the name of the B&B.   Had that really been her own idea, or had Honor suggested it in some way to get her attention?   "You may be right.   But I have no control over what happens, and when. I guess, I'll have to wait and see if she comes to me again.   Thanks Chase, you've been very kind in not thinking I'm being silly.   And I appreciate your input."

Chase sat up straight in surprise.   "Does that mean you forgive me?   For my bad actions earlier, I mean."

Nora laughed. "Of course, just don't drink without eating next time."

Chase looked at her seriously then and said, "In vino veritas."

"What do you mean?" asked Nora.

"In wine there is truth," he said softly. Then he stood up, went over to her. In one fluid motion, he bent down, caressed her cheek, and kissed her gently on the lips. Then he turned and walked out of the room. When he left, it felt to Nora as if the air had left with him.

Chapter Nineteen

Nora had a rough night after Chase had walked out of the room, leaving his kiss on her lips.   First she dreamed of Will, laughing and teasing, always acting silly like a child.   For him it was all about fun.   Then she would dream of Chase, strong dependable, and oh so sexy.   Two totally different men who had become friends as boys and managed to stay that way even with those differences.   At one point, she had opened her eyes after tossing and turning, and she saw Will standing at the end of bed.   It felt very real when she clearly heard him say, "It's okay, Nora. It's okay."   That was it, nothing else, but she felt at peace after that, even though the chance of getting any more sleep was over.

She rose early, made coffee, and then grabbed a tablet to make a list of things she wanted to get done for the day: pay bills, buy groceries, clean drawing room and water plants in sunroom.   She waited and worried, but Chase never came down for breakfast, and when she looked outside, Nora saw that his car was gone.   She assumed that he, too, had had a sleepless night and had left early to avoid her.

The fact was, that even though Chase probably would not have made that move without a little alcohol in his system, he was feeling pretty good.   Being that close to Nora was all he had thought about from the minute he first laid eyes on her, but he always abided by the strict code of all his male friends which was: even after a breakup, not with my woman.   He had actually been feeling guilty about his feelings for Nora after Will's death, but last night something strange had happened. He woke up from a deep sleep, to see Will standing at the foot of his bed, and he was saying, "It's okay, Chase. It's okay." Chase knew what that meant, and he was going to take Will at his word, even after death. He grinned to himself. He would still have to proceed carefully, but now that he had Will's approval, nothing was going to stop him from pursuing Nora.

The phone was ringing off the hook. It seemed like everyone wanted to book a weekend in the middle of winter. Nora would never have thought that she would be busy then. It seemed there was some kind of Winter Fest, with ice fishing, ice sculpting competitions, and snowmobile races. She looked up the festival online on the city's website, and printed off the list of activities in case anyone asked about them. This was the first time she had bookings during the week; she was definitely going to need help in order to keep up with the cleaning.

After unloading the groceries, Nora felt the need for a break. She had never had a chance to walk through her woods and out to the creek, and it was a perfect day for that, even though it was a little nippy. She grabbed her winter coat and wrapped a scarf around her neck. The pond was empty and silent. The swan had stopped coming lately; most likely he had moved on in anticipation of winter. The frogs were no longer croaking, the crickets had been silent for days, and as she began to walk the path in the woods, she noticed that the bird population seemed to have dwindled, also. Nora vowed right then to take more advantage of the outdoors next year. Because of Will's death, she had lost the whole summer and now most of the fall.

The path she was walking was quite pleasant but she could see that the undergrowth had begun to creep in, making it too narrow for two people walking side-by-side. She made a mental note to ask Chase to keep it widened so couples could stroll next to each other, perhaps holding hands. And maybe they would stop for a kiss.

Her woods was filled with exceptionally tall white pines. Obviously, they had been there a long time. She stopped to watch as a cardinal landed on a branch of one. The red and green contrast was beautiful. Nora remembered hearing a story about how the cardinal got its red color and why they remain all winter. The story, as she had been told as a kid, said that some little brown sparrows were perched in a pine tree, softly chirping, waiting for the birth of the baby Jesus. But a strong wind came up and it began to snow heavily. The branches of the pine became heavy with the weight and started to droop. All of the little birds left to go find shelter deeper in the woods or burrow down into the bushes. One little brown bird remained, stubbornly refusing to leave until he heard of the Birth of the King. In the morning, when he awoke, he was completely covered in snow, but when he shook off his feathers, he found that he had turned a beautiful red color, and all of the branches of the pine tree he was perched on were pointing upwards toward Heaven. It was then he knew that the new born King had arrived, and he began to sing his loud clear call that echoed throughout the woods, the call of the cardinal we hear to this day. After hearing that story, Nora had declared the cardinal to be her favorite bird. For her, it was a signal that God was always nearby, listening to her prayers. Oftentimes, when she was distressed, a cardinal would fly right across her path, whether she was walking or driving in the car. Today, she was once again reminded, that God was with her, Will was with Him, and she needed to continue living here while she was still on Earth. There was a peace in her heart that she had not felt in a long, long time.

Soon she came to the small creek that wove through town and then emptied into Lake Michigan. There was a bench on the bank that had been left for couples to sit on, and it was in obvious need of repair. Another thing to ask Chase to take care of. She realized just how much she depended on him now. How could she ever have managed without his help?

She was sitting very quietly watching the ripples of the water as they made their way around a downed tree trunk that had fallen across the stream. The movement was almost hypnotic, and the lapping sound created a steady three-beat rhythm reminding her once again of the Chopin Nocturne that Honor had played on the piano. Nora began to sway slowly to the music in her head, but stopped immediately when a huge bird landed on the fallen tree.

Sitting there not more than 50 or 60 feet away from her was a beautiful bald eagle.   He lifted his wings away from his body as if to air them out, picked at a few feathers, and then turned his majestic head and looked her right in the eye. As soon as he realized he was not alone, he took flight.   Nora jumped up, and shielding her eyes from the sun, tried to follow him.   He soared up and up so high she could only see a small figure, but he continued to glide and dip gracefully, with seemingly no movement of his wings, catching air currents only known to him.   His dance was beautiful to behold, and something she was sure she would never forget in her entire life.

As she was standing, Nora noticed a small path that ran along the creek edge, and it looked so inviting she decided to follow it a little way. Her walk was so enjoyable she dreaded having to go back, but the time had come to return to her duties, so she took another path that was obviously heading back toward the house. Suddenly, she came across a small cemetery with a black wrought iron fence around it, with not more than ten or so tombstones. The entrance to the fenced in area was an arched arbor, very likely done by the same craftsman as the one who had done the gazebo. At the top it simply said "Taylor." Nora stepped over tall grasses and weeds until she came to the stones. Most were so old they were unreadable, the weather having worn away parts of the names and dates, but the largest one clearly said Charles Taylor, 1806-1870. Next to that was one similar in size, and on it Nora was able to read Hannah Horne Taylor, wife and mother, 1816-1875. Just a few feet away were three stones together, one was quite small. Nora brushed away twigs and leaves until she could decipher the weathered script. The first said William Cartwright, May God rest his soul, 1834-1854. Next was Honor's stone, Honora B. Taylor

Cartwright, Loving wife and mother, 1836-1886. Nora was surprised to see the word "mother." So far these were dates that Kate had already discovered, but this small one was new to her. Thomas Peter Taylor, Our Darling Boy, Living with the Angels, February 6, 1855 – August 18, 1855.   Nora suddenly got tears in her eyes when she realized that Honor had not only lost her husband eight months after they were married, but then lost his child, born after William's death.   She counted on her fingers and discovered that the baby had only been six months old at the time of his death.   Nora couldn't imagine the pain Honor must have felt, when the child who was to give her a small piece of her husband forever, had also passed away. This explained the reason for the sorrow that Honor displayed.   Honor had lived to be sixty years of age, and since her last name was Cartwright on the tombstone, it was obvious that she had never remarried.   She must have had a very sad and lonely life.   Nora sank to her knees, tears trickling down her cheeks, and as she sent a prayer to God, she made a promise to her herself that she would care for this cemetery and honor the inhabitants for as long as she was the owner of The Kindred Spirit B&B.

On the walk back to the house, Nora's thoughts were swirling.   She knew she did not have a complete picture of Honor's world yet, but what else was she missing?   As she got closer to the mansion, she was surprised to see Paige waiting for her in the gazebo.

"Hi, what brings you to my part of the world?"

Paige stood up to greet her with a hug. "I just haven't seen you in a while and was wondering how you were."

Nora laughed.   "It's not like we don't talk on the phone almost every day.   But I admit a visit in person is very nice.   Come inside for some coffee.   It's getting colder out.   It looks like we've lost our sun for a while," she said, scanning the sky.   The cloud cover had come in quickly, as it does so often when moving over the Lake.

Just as they closed the door to the kitchen, there was a loud thunderclap and the rain began to pour.   "Wow," said Paige, "we just made it."

"Let me start the coffee, and then we can talk," said Nora.   "I'm sensing some other reason for this visit."

"Not really," responded Paige.   "Just checking in.   How are things going with the B&B?"

Nora kept herself busy getting out the cups, sugar, and cream.   She could tell that Paige was fishing for something.   "Oh, for Pete's sake, Paige, we're too good of friends for us to dance around each other like this. What is it?"

Paige started to say something, stopped herself, and started again. "I don't know why this is so hard for me to say, but it's because I love you both."

"What are you trying to say?"

"Chase told me about the night that he was drunk and kissed you. I was wondering how things are going since that happened. I don't want to see anyone hurt, and I surely don't want to lose my BFF. I can't lose my lughead of a brother; I'm stuck with him, I guess."

"Oh, Paige, don't let it bother you. We haven't. We've moved on."

"But that's just it, Nora. Chase doesn't want to move on. He's in love and you know it."

"In love?" Nora was truly shocked. She had not thought about loving anyone else. "I have to admit to feeling an attraction, a very strong one as a matter of fact.   I think we've both been fighting it.   I chalked it up to loneliness and the fact that an eligible, handsome man is living in my house.   But I had no idea that Chase was feeling love!"

"Well, Nora, don't look so horrified. He's a great guy, and you could do worse. There are all kinds of men who would be ready to prey on a young widow with a business of her own."

Nora laughed.   "It's not like I'm wealthy. I'm barely making it by, as a matter of fact."

Paige pushed her napkin around in circles, trying to think about how to say the rest. "Nora, you're the best friend I've ever had, and you know we say that we are each other's kindred spirits.   I don't want to lose you, if this doesn't work out.   Chase can look cocky sometimes and act like a ladies' man, but the truth is, he hasn't dated one single girl since you came to town."

"What?" Nora was shocked. She had seen him with any number of women when they went out as a group. He would move from table to table talking with all of his friends who were mostly female. "No one? Not even when Will was still alive?"

"No one. I think he felt something for you the minute he laid eyes on you. He's very protective, you know. I'm fully aware of his gift, or whatever it is, and I know he probably knew you would be having a tough go of it soon. He instinctively wanted to be there for you. And for a man, there's nothing more enticing than feeling needed."

Nora reached across the table and took Paige's hand. She could sense the distress her friend was feeling. "Don't worry, Paige. I could never hurt him. I'm not sure if I am ready for a relationship yet, but I have to admit to feeling a very strong attraction toward Chase. We've actually confided in each other about a few things, and it's brought us a lot closer together.   But no matter what happens, I won't let it come between you and me.   You've been there for me through thick and thin, and I would never let our friendship fall apart."

"That does make me feel better.   Thank you for putting me at ease."

"Paige, I do have a request of you, so I'm glad you stopped by."

"What is it?   I'll be glad to help you with anything, you know that."

"Well, I've told you all about the Taylor family tree, and I'm sure Kate has filled you in, as well.   I'm starting to see a picture of what this founding family was like, but there are still some pieces missing.   Would you be able to go to the museum with me?   I understand they have a room dedicated to the Taylors and their influence on the community.   I'm not much of a museum person, and I guess I just wanted a companion."

Paige took a sip of her coffee, then set it down when she realized it was still too hot.   "I'd love to go.   I know the curator, Mrs. Sandford, very well.   She's been collecting artifacts and clippings for years."

"Great!   Do you think we could go tomorrow?   I already looked up their hours, and I see that tomorrow night is the one night of the week that they're open in the evening. Could we go after your shop closes?"

"It's a deal.   I'll come by and pick you up. About 7?

"Perfect.   Now let's talk about quilting, makeup, or anything else girlie.   I need to get my head out of the past for a little while."

Chapter Twenty

The bell jingled as the girls walked into the museum. There was a small stand with a sign-in sheet for visitors, and next to it was a jar for a free-will offering. Paige explained that the town taxes helped a little to keep the museum open, but the donations were crucial to the acquisition of new artifacts. Nora knew only too well about keeping a business running and trying to pay expenses, so she stuffed in a five dollar bill.

Soon an older woman of about sixty or more came out to greet them. Paige said hello, and then introduced her to Nora. They explained the purpose for their visit; so Mrs.

Sandford, or Betty as she asked them to call her, led them straight to a room displaying pictures of the early settlers.   The wall was lined with old black and white shots of the lumberyard that the Taylors had run.   Some showed the forest that the laborers were cutting down.   The loggers sported long beards and wore pants and suspenders.   A few men held crosscut saws in their hands as they posed for the group pictures. One man had his leg propped up on a tree stump, while resting his arm on his leg.   He held a smoking pipe in the other hand, his hat perched on his head at a jaunty angle.

They found an article that had been written for an early settler's book in 1937, the year of Michigan's centennial.   Paige read aloud to Nora as it described how Charles Taylor had come from Canada to settle the territory of Michigan which was trying to become a state. In order to be ratified as one of the states of the United States of America, territories had to meet a population requirement, so Michigan offered free land to homesteaders.   This was a common practice in that time period, and it brought people from all areas looking for fresh start. After Charles Taylor claimed his allotted amount of land, he began to buy up neighboring parcels at a very low price.   Soon his land holdings numbered in the thousands of acres.   His log business brought men who were looking for jobs, and a town formed to support the workers and their families.   It wasn't long, the article said, before Charles Taylor soon had control of the bank, the hardware store, and the mercantile. In other words, he owned everything necessary for life.   The article explained how he then branched out to the shipping business running from Chicago to Sioux St. Marie, in order to ship his lumber to other cities and even other parts of the world.   It was no wonder that his mansion was so beautiful.   He was a very wealthy man. Michigan finally had enough citizens to become the 26th state in the Union in 1837, only five years after the Taylors had arrived.

"Wow, this is unbelievable," said Nora, "how a man could become a millionaire so quickly. I have a feeling, though, that he already had some money when he arrived; otherwise how else would he have been able to buy that amount of acreage? Very interesting, but it doesn't give me the information I was hoping for." She glanced around and saw nothing else of interest to her at this time. "What's in that next room?"

"This is the maritime room," said Paige. "In case you didn't know, Lake Michigan has quite a reputation for shipwrecks, even to present time. There are people who come here from all over the world to study these maps. Some have spent a small fortune looking for old ships and their bounty that sank hundreds of years ago. People are still diving, to this day, looking for gold doubloons. Every once in a while someone gets lucky and finds a ship at the bottom of the Lake."

"Look at this map with all the pegs where ships have gone down. What is this red line that forms a triangle on the map?" Nora leaned in to read the placard. "It says, 'Lake Michigan has a triangle that has been compared to the Bermuda Triangle and is just as deadly. Many ships and boats have gone missing or had strange accidents in that area. The line runs from Ludington to Benton Harbor to Manitowoc, Wisconsin.' Wow, I never heard of this before."

"Yes," said Paige, "and we're right in that area. It's one of the reasons tourists come this way, besides the dunes and the fishing and hunting, of course."

"Paige, look at this. An article about a particular shipwreck that happened right near the Platte Bay."

"Oh, you must mean the Westmoreland. It's one of the local history stories that we learned about in school.   Here.   Here's a photocopy of a newspaper article about it.   You can take it with you if you like."

Nora began to read, and was stunned. The date of the disaster was Dec.7, 1854, the exact same date as William Cartwright's death. Could there be a connection?   It was too much of a coincidence.   She read out loud the account of the shipwreck, starting part-way down the article.   It had been copied from an article printed in 2010 in The Grand Rapids Press.

"At 10 a.m. on December 7, 1854, rising water in the bilge finally extinguished the fire in the boiler, leaving the cargo-laden steamer powerless and thrown to the mercy of the heavy, icy seas off a then-remote stretch of Lake Michigan coastline.

"Half the souls on board would soon perish in the deep, frigid waters of Platte Bay.

The other half would spread the legend of a ship reputed to be carrying $100,000 in gold coins in her safe and 280 barrels of whiskey in her hold, sparking more than a century of treasure hunters that would search in vain for the wreck.

"The ship which left Chicago before stopping in Milwaukee, was headed to Mackinac Island with supplies of oats, flour, grass seed, wool, butter, hogs, lard, and beef.   It was the last run of the year ---- speculation over the years was that the Westmoreland was on a payroll run for the army garrison there.   The gold in the form of $20 double eagle pieces, and the whiskey, was supposedly loaded in Chicago.

"Stories tell of a small, drunken party of German lumberjacks who locked themselves in their cabin playing cards when the storm hit and soused themselves on the cargo whiskey, eventually being left behind when the crew abandoned ship.

"The ship was heavily laden with cargo and burdened with a thick ice coating from the waves. It sprung a leak mid-lake. Captain Thomas Clark tried to make safe harbor at South Manitou, but the boilers were doomed within sight of the protective harbor. Powerless, the steamer, sinking at the stern, began to drift south through the treacherous Manitou Passage."

Nora skipped down the page a little and continued to read. "One of the surviving crew members described the chaotic attempts to load the lifeboats in this December 24, 1854 Buffalo Morning News article describing how the stern of the boat went under first, and as the ship listed to starboard, a lifeboat flipped more than a dozen people into the swirling icy waters.

"The sounds of the stern were deafening. People were yelling and screaming and the whines and howls of William Saltonstall's sled dogs could be heard as the Westmoreland

slipped beneath the waves.   Several of the men
who were tossed from the large lifeboat were
last seen clinging to the arches as the
Westmoreland foundered.   The icy seas
bubbled with white foam and wreckage from
the cabins and anything else buoyant enough to
rip itself off the ship.   The 15 passengers and
crew who were left behind either drowned or
quickly froze to death in the frigid water."

Nora stopped reading a moment as the
reality of what had happened sank in.   "It goes
on to say, that the two surviving lifeboats landed
on shore a quarter mile east of the Platte River
mouth, then a remote dune river winding
through a stretch of giant virgin pine trees.   The
17 survivors split into groups making for
Mackinac and Traverse City by hugging the
coastline."

"I've heard about this shipwreck all of my
life," said Paige, "but until now, I've never really

327

thought about how terrible it was.   Reading about it as an adult makes it so much more real."

Nora was looking at a brass plaque on the wall next to a diorama of the ship.   It was a list of those who had perished in the disaster.   She traced her finger down until it rested on the name she already knew she would find – William Cartwright.   Just as she had thought when she first started reading, Honor's husband was on that ship and was one of the unfortunate souls who had not survived.   She knew exactly the agony that Honor had gone through.   She could feel her pain.   And even though it was 160 years later, she could hear Honor crying out for her husband when she first heard the news. Nora covered her eyes with her hands and joined in with cries of her own.

On the drive home Paige had been respectfully quiet, waiting for Nora to calm

herself.   She knew that hearing of another's
woman's husband passing away in an accident
on Lake Michigan must have been very difficult
for Nora.   When they arrived at the B&B, Nora
didn't get out of the car immediately because she
wanted to explain a few things to Paige.   She
told her about finding the cemetery, and how the
dates of the shipwreck had coordinated with the
tombstone markings, and she also told her that
Honor had lost a child after her husband died.
Nora tried her best to help Paige understand
why her emotions had been so raw, but there
was no need.   Paige fully understood, and had
already decided not to press the issue.   Nora
realized that Paige was a good friend, in all ways,
and was a true kindred spirit; and she also now
understood that through time, somehow, Honor
had also become her kindred spirit.   Later that
night while rehashing everything in her mind
that happened since she first arrived in Taylor
Ridge, she understood that Honor had been

trying to tell her that life was meant for living. Honor had lived the rest of her days alone.   She had nieces and nephews through her brother, which had then become Chase's family line, and maybe she didn't feel quite so lonely because of that, but Nora knew from her own experience, that nothing would ever replace the love she had felt for her husband.   Nora also knew that she, herself, had a long life ahead of her, if God was willing, and if she were to ever remarry, she would have more time on Earth with a second husband than she had been granted with her first.   The reality of what everyone had been telling her set in; that life moves on whether we want it to or not, and we must make the most of the time we have.   Honor had been showing Nora her misery in hopes that Nora would come through her darkness into the light and find new hope and happiness.

After that day, Nora's attitude about a lot

of things changed.   The ache would always be there, she was sure, but with time she knew it would lessen and perhaps even go away for a little while.   But she also knew she would never forget Will, never.   He would always have a piece of her heart, but there was room for someone else now, and when the time was right, she knew she was ready.

The days passed quickly with B&B traffic that Nora had not experienced to this point. She was either shopping, cleaning, cooking or answering phones.   The snow had started to fall early in November, and for some reason this year it never quit.   Chase was always gone when she got up in the morning, trying to keep up with the plowing.   There were some days when the bad roads had caused cancellations, but for the most part, the hardy souls of Michigan just kept coming.   They spent more time outside than

Nora ever would have. She was amazed at the desire for people to experience the cold, wet outdoors.

Chase spent most evenings at home with her. If they had guests, they sat in her kitchen, having snacks, or in the back of the house, watching TV or a movie. It was easy being with Chase, because he knew everything about her and her visions.

Nora never saw Honor again after that day at the museum. It seemed as though Honor had decided that her mission was done. Maybe she was still there watching, but Nora never even felt her presence.

As the time for Christmas drew near, Chase helped her with the decorations, and he put up the trees after she had asked him to pick up a small one for the foyer, and a second one for the parlor. One night, when no one else was in the house, they played Christmas music and trimmed the trees. Nora found herself laughing freely as they reached out to hang ornaments on the same branch.   When Chase climbed the ladder to hang the treetop, Nora's eyes began to study his physic.   He was lean, with firm, tight muscles from all of the outdoor work.   She had certainly never heard him mention going to a gym or doing any jogging.   Because of the physical activity in his line of work, lifting weights and walking on a treadmill wasn't necessary.   As he reached for the top of the tree, Nora studied the curve from his bicep to his forearm, then her eyes went to his neck and his broad shoulders.   She suddenly had an overwhelming desire to run her hands down his back.   When he turned around to ask if the star was placed correctly, he caught the flush on her cheeks.   He took a moment to stare at her lovely face, hoping that what he had been praying for was finally beginning to happen. Nora smiled at him and then lowered her eyes to the box of ornaments in her hand.   It had been but a brief exchange through the eyes, but one that gave a simple message of the beginning stages of courtship, and Chase was thrilled beyond belief.

Later, when their work was complete, and they had admired everything they had accomplished, they sat by the fire drinking hot chocolate. This time Nora sat next to Chase on the loveseat. He carefully placed his arm on the back of the sofa, waiting a moment to see if she would object, and when she didn't pull away, he slowly slid his arm down to encompass her shoulders. He thought he heard her sigh, or maybe the sigh had come from him. They sat in silence for a few moments watching the flames crackle and flicker as in a lover's dance, much in the same manner they had been dancing around each other over the past few months.

Finally, Nora felt as if something had to be said.   "Chase, we've come a long way, haven't we?"

Chase squeezed her a little, and said, "That we have.   'It was the best of times; it was the worst of times,' as Charles Dickens said. But I'm glad I could be there for you."

Nora cleared her throat trying to stall for a few moments, while she got ready to say what needed to be said.   "This has been wonderful, the Christmas decorating and all, I mean.   And while we've been busy singing carols and putting greens on the banisters, I've felt us grow closer."

"What are you trying to say, Nora?" Chase began to experience panic at the idea that she was about to put up a wall between them.

"It's just that it's all quite wonderful, and I feel comfortable with this new-found closeness, but I'm wondering if it's a good idea, now, for us to be living together."

"Nora, I'm the same man I've always been.   If you must know, I've had feelings for you since the day we met.   If I was going to do something inappropriate, it would have happened a long time ago."

Nora sat up a little and pulled away from his protective arm.   "I guess I thought that was the case, but I wasn't sure -- about your feelings, I mean.   What I'm trying to say is, do you think we can keep a business relationship going on, here, and not ruin what has started to happen between us?   Because, I sort of like it."   She teased him with a smile.

Chase looked into those golden cat eyes and said softly, "I tell you what, I'll do my best to be a perfect gentleman, but that doesn't mean I'm going to keep my hands off of you, altogether."   And since he felt more secure with what was happening between them, he pulled her in for a kiss.   This time it was not a gentle kiss on the lips, like it had been the night he was drunk, but a long, tender kiss of someone who was finally able to show his love. Her lips were soft and matched his perfectly as she responded back with more passion than he had expected. This time he was *sure* the sigh was his own.

Chapter Twenty-one

The snow continued to fall throughout January and February in what was to be the snowiest winter in years. Towards the end of February, even seasoned Michiganders were getting tired of it and ready for spring. After the Winter Fest in January, bookings began to go downhill, and the B&B was struggling. Nora was sure that things would come around again as soon as the weather got better, but she wasn't sure if she could hold on until that happened. March was traditionally spring break month, and the time when everyone went south, not north to the woods and dunes. The strain of having to keep up with the bills was beginning to show on her face, and Chase noticed.   He decided it was time to have the talk that he had been wanting for months, now.

It was Sunday morning, and without guests to serve, Nora just made bacon and eggs. The two of them sat at the table like an old couple, one with the newspaper, and one with a magazine.   Finally Chase said, "Nora, I have an idea.   I've been thinking about it for quite some time, but I didn't think you would be ready to hear it.   Do you mind if we talk about it?"

Nora looked up, put her magazine down, and said, "Of course, what's on your mind?"

"Well," said Chase hesitantly, "I've noticed that you seem to be preoccupied a lot lately, and I thought you might be having trouble keeping up with the mortgage without a steady flow of paying guests."

"Yes, I am preoccupied, but it's not the mortgage.   It's the heating bill.   I had no idea it would soar that high.   I don't know what I'm going to do, unless I take my savings down to the last cent, and then what will I have left?"   Tears sprang to her eyes which just made her angry at herself.   She didn't like appearing as a weak female unable to take care of herself.

"I have a proposition for you, if you'd like to hear it."   He went on not waiting for her answer.   "I'm pretty tired of the snow plowing business.   I love landscaping and gardening, but I really have never been much for the snow and cold.   And getting up at the crack of dawn to plow is wearing me down."

"What are you thinking?" asked Nora.

"I have a nice little savings account.   I'd like to buy into the bed-and-breakfast business, at whatever percentage you'd like.   I'm willing to go fifty-fifty, but if you don't want to sell that much of the B&B, I understand.   I'd give up plowing, except for our own drive, of course. Eventually, I would give up the landscaping business, too, and dedicate myself to this place.

I could be your full time handyman and yardman. I'd be able to help with the heavy duty cleaning, with the things that you can't reach, or I could help move furniture that is too heavy. I have a few other ideas, also, but let's start there. Any thoughts?"

"Oh, Chase, my first instinct is to hold on for dear life because it's what Will wanted, but he isn't here, and honestly, I'm floundering. I think a fifty-fifty deal sounds wonderful. It certainly would bail me out, and it's far more acceptable to selling."

"You accepted quicker than I thought you would! Thank you, Nora. It means a lot to me; I like the idea of being a part owner of my ancestors' home. When would you like to do this?"

"Let's go to the bank and a lawyer to make everything legal. How about calling someone tomorrow? I know it will probably take a while to get all of the papers signed."

"Wonderful.   Until then, I'd like to pay your heating bill.   We wouldn't want them to turn it off; we might have to snuggle more closely, then."   They shook hands formally, then laughed, and went in to seal it with a kiss. And then there were a few more kisses for good measure.

Chase kept up with the plowing to honor his clients until the end of the season, but as soon as April came, he gave notice that he would not be available for them next year.   He spent his days outside, raking, trimming bushes, planting more bulbs and annuals.   With his creativity in the yard, the grounds were becoming glorious.   He even began to work on the greenhouse.   He said it was an eyesore and whether they used it or not it should at least look decent.   He ripped down vines, cleaned out years of junk that had been stored in it, and replaced and cleaned windows, making sure they opened and closed properly to allow heat and humidity to either be trapped inside on cold days, or to escape in the summer when the hot sun raised the temperature too much for the plants. Chase had never been happier -- except for one thing, he still had to make Nora his, but only when she was ready. It was getting more and more difficult for him to wait.

In May, Paige helped put on a quilt expo at the school gym, and along with that she also gave some classes and brought speakers in to give seminars. Nora had no idea that quilting was such a big business. She had always just quilted on her own from magazine patterns she found or books she had purchased. She had never been to a quilt show in her life, and she was not able to go this time, either, which was disappointing, because her B&B was packed. Every room had at least two women in it, and in some cases, they'd had to bring in cots for a third, because there was not one more room available in town, even at Mr. Reed's motel. There was never a seat empty at the Lite House or any of the other local restaurants.   So overall, the quilt show had been good business for everyone.   Nora had actually had to put Chase to work in the kitchen at times to help out there.   He was great with the ladies, some of them quite enjoying his flirtatious manner as he checked them in.   When it was over, Nora realized that she had made him partner just in time.   She appreciated him more and more each day.

Then all of sudden it was June, and Kate and Conor's wedding was just around the corner. Nora had already met with the wedding planner they had selected; she was very nice and seemed easy to get along with.   Kate was taking care of everything on her end by Skype, Facetime, and texting.   She trusted her planner completely, and was prepared to just show up with her bridesmaid, Conor's sister, Ellen, and get ready at the B&B.   Nora, she was told, only had to take care of guests the same as always.   The wedding planner would bring in the flowers and decorations, and the tents and chairs for the yard, as they still planned to get married in the gazebo by the pond.   Nora was told that it was to be immediate family only.   Since Kate had no one on her side to invite, as she was estranged from her sister, Conor's family would make up the rest of the guest list, including Paige and Ted, and Chase, who was to be the best man.

Finally the wedding day neared.   Nora was nervous.   What if something went wrong?   Would they blame her for it?   She and Chase had been in a cleaning frenzy, and they were both exhausted.   It was a beautiful early summer evening so they decided to take a glass of wine out to the gazebo and try to relax before the big day tomorrow.

"Look at the stars," said Nora. "Until I moved to Taylor Ridge I had never seen anything like this."

"It's especially beautiful in the middle of the night when all house and store lights are off," commented Chase. "Hey, do you want to get on the paddle boat? I haven't seen you use it yet."

"As a matter of fact, I was thinking about that the last time I was out here. "Let's go." And she started to run toward the pond.

Chase had never seen Nora run and act carefree like a child before. It was over a full year now, since Will's death, and every day he could see some of her sadness slipping away. He was happy for her. It seemed as if she was finally moving through the last stages of grief. Nora kicked off her sandals and they stepped onto the dock. Chase untied the boat, then held her hand as she climbed into her seat. They easily maneuvered the small craft out to the middle of the pond, where they let the boat drift as they studied the stars.   They sat in silence, holding hands, and wondered at the beauty of nature.   Finally Nora said, "God is good, Chase. I've been truly blessed to have been able to own this property."

"And I am just as blessed to have you in my life and to be a part of this property, also." Did he dare, he wondered?   Was the time finally right?   "Nora, I feel like I was meant to be here, with you, in this place, to help you run the B&B.   But it's more than that.   I love you. I love you more than words can say.   I can truly say that I have never felt this way in my life."

Chase realized that, as soon as he finished talking, he began holding his breath.   Nora was staring at his face as if a struggle was going on inside her.   She had a brief moment of panic when Chase first said he loved her, but suddenly a vision of Honor came to her mind; the pain and agony of losing both a husband and a child was the same pain she had felt.   Then a vision of Will flashed before her – he was laughing and saying, "Come on Nora, just do it!" just like when he had tried to convince her to buy this place. She was sure then that she had his approval. He had put her in his best friend's hands, to be cared for and loved. And to love him in return. Everything was going to be okay from now on.

She looked at Chase's eyes, his hair, then down to his hands. Her thumb made a steady motion as she caressed his, then she looked up with tears in her eyes, and her smile produced a radiance he had not seen on her face before. "I love you, too, Chase Phillips. I love you."

They tried to kiss but the separation of the seats made it difficult, so as they laughed with joy, they quickly paddled to the dock, and jumped out. Under the moon and all of the stars of Taylor Ridge, they shared a kiss, and then another and another. Chase pulled Nora's body in close so that it fit perfectly with his.

And as they walked toward the gazebo, he knew he had never been happier in his entire life.

Chapter Twenty-two

Nora woke up in a panic.   It was the wedding day, and they would all be arriving soon.   Could she do this?   Would she be able to keep her cool and hold everything together? She took a deep breath and tried to remember that it was all in the hands of Mary, the wedding planner.   Nora went immediately to the window and looked up at the clear sky.   Not a cloud in sight, so far.   This was Michigan after all, where the weather could change on a dime.   There was a saying that goes, 'if you don't like the weather, wait a minute'; and Nora had discovered this was actually true.   But for now all reports from the weatherman was for a perfect 75-degree day with no wind.

She showered and dressed quickly, opting for something quite casual until the time when she would change into a dress for the wedding. Since she was dating Chase now and he was family, she was to be seated with the guests, and not just on the sidelines as the owner of the B&B as she had originally thought, so she would have no choice but to let others run the show.

Suddenly the doorbell was ringing and Nora could hear voices outside.   When she opened the door she heard Mary say, "take everything out back first and then we'll arrange it."   She spun back to Nora, "Good morning! We're here, and it's my favorite day of the year. A wedding day!"

Nora said, "You sound eager to get started.   Feel free to make the kitchen your headquarters, and there is a restroom right over there for any of your helpers."

"Thank you, Nora.   Now you go relax. I've got this all under control."   And that she did.   They raised the tent canopy and spaced out the chairs to perfection.   The guests were to sit under the canopy while the bride and groom were married in the gazebo.   There were flowers placed on stands and tables with glasses for punch and other beverages.   Decorations and lights hung from trees branches.   The food would come out after the ceremony.

Kate and Ellen arrived a few hours later. "Nora, I want you to meet, Conor's sister, Ellen. She's a librarian, also, and she helped with some of the genealogy for you."

Ellen had long dark hair and shocking blue eyes, just like her brother's.   She was a vision and would make a lovely bridesmaid. "It's so nice to meet you.   I enjoyed doing the family tree, and I learned the basics from Kate as we went along, so it was also educational for me."

"Then, thank you, for your work."

Kate's hair had already been done up in a sweep with a few curls. Neither one had any makeup on yet. Nora could see they were carrying bags with shoes and all the incidentals a bride would need. She told them she would get some help with the dresses, and bring them up shortly.

And then they began arriving a carload at a time. Conor came with Bart, Ellen's husband, and his father, Eric McAuley. He was a jolly man who walked with a slight limp and used a cane.

Next came Audrey Doane and Gus Adams, who had previously stayed at the B&B, so Nora felt she knew them well already. They were with their friends, Melody and Nick Gianopoulos, who had also been guests. It was obvious that Melody was pregnant, and she beamed as she whispered in Nora's ear that conception had happened on their weekend at the Kindred Spirit.   And the relatives just kept coming and coming, and Nora thought how nice it was to have a large and happy family.   One elderly couple, Patrick and Louella McAuley, came with a friend, who had driven them all the way from South Haven, they said.   They introduced themselves as Audrey's grandparents, and Conor's great aunt and uncle on his father's side.

Chase arrived already dressed in his tux, and Nora had never seen him look more handsome.   In fact, she had never seen him dressed in anything other than jeans and work shirts or tees.   She had no idea he could clean up so good, and she told him so.

And then it was time for everyone to be seated.   The music started signaling that it was time for Kate to walk down the white carpet. Suddenly, the music changed to a classical piece, one that Kate and Conor had chosen together. Nora gasped when she heard the beginning strains of Chopin's Nocturne #2, Opus number 9, in E flat Major.   She looked at Chase and saw that he only had eyes for her, even though he was supposed to be watching the wedding party.

And finally it was time for Ellen to begin walking down the aisle.   She was wearing a summery yellow, chiffon dress, and carrying white roses.   And then Kate began the walk towards her groom, who was looking a little uncomfortable in his tuxedo, but excited none the less, especially when his eyes fell on the beautiful Kate.   She was wearing an ivory dress with simple lines, and she had a lace veil simply draped over her head.   The effect with her skin color and auburn hair was breathtaking.   Her yellow bouquet was the exact opposite color combination of Ellen's.   The photographer snapped multiple pictures as they said their vows, and in what seemed like a very short time it was over, and the bride and groom were kissing.   Everyone cheered, and clapped.   They were a very exuberant and joyful family, and obviously an outdoor wedding was just the right venue for them.

There wasn't a formal reception line, everyone just took their turn to greet the new couple as husband and wife. Nora waited to make her way over to them when she was sure the family had all had a chance.

"Congratulations. It was a beautiful wedding."

"Thanks to you, Nora. We loved getting married here" said Kate. "It was absolutely perfect."

"We'll be sure to pass this on to others if you want us to," said Conor, as he gave her a hug. "Now, what's up with you and Chase? Any chance you might join the family?"

"Conor!" Kate gave him a little punch.

"That's okay," laughed Nora. "We're taking it one day at a time. It's all pretty new right now."

"Well, I for one am praying for you, Nora. You deserve it," added Kate.

"I will, too, but when does the party start?" asked Conor.

"Right now, you big lug." laughed Kate. "Let's go.   They're calling us for our first dance."   The beginning strains of Nora Jones singing The Nearness of You began playing, and the couple danced with their bodies pressed closely together, on a dance floor which had been set up on the perfectly-manicured, green grass.

It's not the pale moon that excites me,
That thrills and delights me
Oh no
It's just the nearness of you.

And then as soon as that song was completed, the music changed to the more upbeat tempo of Up a Lazy River.

Chase grabbed Nora's hand and spun her out to the center of the floor, then twirled her in a spin.   She had no idea he could move like that.   She had a lot to learn about this man, yet, but she could tell it was going to be a lovely adventure.   As she danced nearer to the bride and groom, she heard Kate tell someone, "I knew the moment that I found out he was a fan of Hoagy Carmichael that he was the man for me." And they all laughed, in what seemed to be an inside joke.

After everyone had gone home, and the yard had been cleaned up by the workers that had been hired for that purpose, Nora and Chase sat in the gazebo, with their arms wrapped around each other.   She was leaning with her back to his chest, watching as the setting sun made beautiful colors on the pond.

Chase whispered in her ear, "Nora, I know the bride is supposed to be the most beautiful woman of the day, but for me it was you.   Just you."

Nora swiveled around to kiss him and when they came up for air, she said, "And you, mister, are drop-dead gorgeous in a tux.   Not many men can pull that look off.   Except maybe your cousin Conor."   She winked.

"Kate and Conor sure were happy, weren't they?   Nora, do you think that could be us someday soon?"

She smiled at him, kissed him again, and swiveled back around into his arms.   "It sure could, Chase.   It sure could."

Chase started to tremble, because he suddenly knew what he wanted to say, and he had not planned it out thoroughly.   He kicked himself for not taking the time to get the words right first.   "Nora, I love you," he said into her hair.   "I have since the day I first set eyes on you.   There's never going to be anyone for me but you, and I promise I will always be there for you."   Then he turned her around again so he could look into her eyes, as he said, "I never thought I could be this happy.   I've been wanting to ask you this for quite a while, now. Would you do me the honor of–"

And at that exact moment a swan came swooping down to the pond.   He glided to the water without a sound, making barely a ripple. "Chase, look," she whispered.   And then, miraculously, a few seconds later, a second swan followed, and settled on the glass-like water. The two birds moved silently side-by side, almost in a lover's dance of their own, and then Nora and Chase watched in awe as they bent their heads, touched them together, and formed a heart shape with their long necks.

""Chase, I think Honor and William are finally happy, and they're together again after 160 years.   I believe those swans are a sign, maybe from Honor, or maybe they're from Will, so if you're asking what I thought you were about to ask a moment ago, the answer is yes, Chase Phillips, I will marry you."

Chase's heart swelled to bursting as he said over and over again, "I love you, Nora.   I love you so much."

They sat for a while watching the swans, and even though the musical equipment had long ago been packed up and removed from the premises, Nora could have sworn that, off in the distance, she heard Chopin's Nocturne, and she knew, beyond a doubt, that it was being played just for them.

Acknowledgments

Although every person and place in this story is a figment of my imagination, the story about the Westmoreland shipwreck is not. On December 7, 1854 the Westmoreland did, indeed, go down off the shores of Lake Michigan near Platte Bay. William Cartwright was not on that ship as he is just a fictional character in my book, but 15 people did lose their lives on that cold and stormy day.

The exact number of shipwrecks that have taken place in Lake Michigan is unknown, but the estimate is that over 6,000 ships sit at the bottom of the Great Lakes to this day, and from the 1600s to this date, approx. 30,000 people have lost their lives.

The article that Nora read at the local museum is an actual article taken from the Grand Rapids Press on November 9, 2014, and the description of what actually happened was from an article in the Buffalo Morning News on December 24, 1854.

It was widely reported that the Westmoreland carried over $100,000 in gold coins in the safe, and this, of course, has attracted the interest of many shipwreck hunters from around the world. On July 7, 2010 a Grand Rapids man by the name of Ross Richardson finally accomplished what others had been unable to do to this point. He discovered the Westmoreland 200 feet below the surface, sitting upright, near the Sleeping Bear Dunes area. He claims it to be the most well-preserved 1850s shipwreck on the planet.

Richardson has since written a book called The Search for the Westmoreland, Lake

364

Michigan's Treasure Shipwreck.   It can be found on Amazon.

For more articles on the shipwrecks of the Great Lakes, you can go to the online site of mlive.com, written by Garret Ellison on Nov. 14, 2012, Nov. 9, 2014, and Feb. 23, 2015.

Some shipwreck websites that may be of interest are:

michiganshipwrecks.org

michiganpreserves.org